I0703822

**Love and Other Pyrrhic Victories**

Aurora Rain Llydell

© 2024  Aurora Rain Llydell



**Published by:**
Bryson Publishing
Kansas City, MO

**Cover Design :** Nathaniel Kreeger

**ISBN:** 978-1-959665-37-3

Love & Other Pyrrhic Victories

A collection of flash fiction and short stories

By Aurora Rain Llydell

To Carmen, who helped curb my insanity with movie marathons.

## Love



## Pyrrhic Victories

# **Love**

## *Old Souls*

The All-Saints Inn was just starting to fill with late risers and tourists when those black coats arrived. The double doors swung open with hardly a sound, but it might as well have been a cannon clap for all the fear it caused. Three men entered, two lingering by the doorway as the third made his way to the counter. The soft, dull thud of his limp on the old wood floors was the only noise. The nimble man leaned an elbow on the bar, his sharp eyes offsetting the lopsided grin on his face.

"Bartholomew, mate!" He said in an easy tone "How's it going for you? Business is good?" The stocky bartender winced as his name was called, and subtly motioned for his wife to retreat to the back.

"It's been slow, but business is business, Oz." He replied, forcing a smile. Oz raked a gloved hand through his short black hair, looking around the Inn.

"Don't I know it," He returned his gaze to Bartholomew, "But you're late on your payment, mate. Gotta say the old man is getting impatient." He leaned further over the counter, locking eyes with the bartender. "Not sure I'll be able to satisfy him with just a few fingers this time." Bartholomew tensed, thinking of his mutilated son.

"N-no! Listen, listen, I have the whole payment, plus interest, alright? Just leave my family out of this." Ozwald made a lazy shooing motion with one hand. "Get on it, then. What are you standing around chatting for?" As the man hurried away Oz turned his attention to the hushed patrons. Showing off his lopsided smile again he announced "Sorry 'bout this here, folks. You'll be able to go back to your meals in just a moment." No one met his eyes. Bartholomew returned with a bulging coin purse. Oz motioned one of his lackeys forward and handed the purse off to be counted.

"It's as he said." The man rumbled, handing the money back to Oz. He looked to the bartender, who was wringing his apron between his hands. He clapped his shoulder, making Bartholomew jump and spoke. "There we go, mate. That wasn't so hard, was it?" He straightened and headed back towards the door, stashing the purse in the pocket of his black trench coat. He stopped just before the exit and looked over his shoulder with a devilish smile. "Good luck, Barty! Your good business is our good business. Right?" With that, the doors swung shut. Throwing a glance over his shoulder, Oz saw both of his black-clad men following ten paces behind. Satisfied, he set his eyes back to scanning the road.

Shadows were beginning to slither out from the cramped alleyways, though it was barely noon. Despite the cold and looming weather, the slums of Avr'rye were still annoyingly crowded. Gambling dens and pleasure houses had hordes of people milling around outside, waiting to be admitted. The breath of streetside vendors began to cloud the air as much as their voices, but nonetheless they hollered themselves hoarse. Once colorful banners now covered in grime and paint assaulted the eyes from all angles, dirtied by the endless streams of soot that poured from every slanted chimney.

"Quickly! Away from the street, child." The locals corralled their young inside moving out of the trio's way when they spotted the ebony trench coats.

"Beware those men if you want your head to stay put..." Whispers swirled through the dull clamor of voices, trailing on his heels as closely as the stares pinned to his back.

"The Ravens are out."

Pushing his way through the thinning crowd, Oz buried his nose into the thin, green scarf wound around his neck, wishing he could do the same to warm his numbing ears. The tourists eyed him with interest, but his men made sure no one got any ideas. Finally, he had made his way to the rich purple door of the Psychic's place. Entering with the bell's soft tinkle, he sighed heavily at the heat that flowed into his bones. It was much darker inside than it was outdoors, but as his visits became more frequent Oz had found it more of a comforting darkness.

The windows were covered with thick curtains and the mosaiced oil lamps that swung from the ceiling sent rainbow fragments scattering across the room. A round table draped in glittering patterned silks claimed the room's center. A crystal ball, a hand painted globe, and a deck of tarot cards sat atop it. A deep, cushy chair was positioned on either end. Beaded pillows scattered light across the room like fallen stars. Shelves bedecked one wall, full of shining crystal vials, incense, worn leather tomes and charms. Charts decorated the other three---palm reading, astronomy, tarot meanings and even a city map. The large stone fireplace built into the far wall roared, executing any lingering chill the customers may have brought in.

Coming farther into the space, Oz leaned on the hearth, putting his hands out to the fire. He turned his head at the soft clinking of the beaded curtain being pulled aside.

"Oh, Che, it's jus' you." said a relieved voice. The woman who'd entered pulled off the headdress and veil that hid her face, long copper curls spilling out over her freckled shoulders.

His lips curled into a smile, "What, I don't get the whole performance?" She shot him a venomous look, as she braided her hair, taking a seat. Ozwald laughed, this woman was the only one in the whole of the slums--the whole of Avr'rye, even--who would dare look at him that way. He took his usual seat, just across the table in a plush chair that smelled faintly of whisky. The flickering light revealed dark circles under the teller's eyes, and her fair skin was paler than usual, her freckles stood out more. And maybe it was just his imagination, but it almost looked like her tunic was a little loose.

Her olive eyes seemed to know he was about to ask, because her lithe hands were already shuffling the tarot cards. "Birds o' a feather may flock t'gether, but a gatherin' of crows is called murder." she said, the slightly sharp tone in her alluring voice wiping the query from his mind. They'd made a silent agreement the night of his first appointment: Ask me no questions and I'll tell you no lies. No names exchanged, no personal queries. Better for business, both ways.

"What brings such darkness to my door?" Mesmerized by her rhythmic shuffling, Oz didn't look up as he said,

"Just part of the schedule, love." Her hands froze, and his obsidian eyes rose to meet hers. A thin copper brow had risen in disbelief, her painted lips forming a frown. "We both know that's not true, Che. Tector doesn't ever see Crow's near here this time o' the month." He winced, then stiffened, feeling something slide through his feet. Outed by the damned snake.

A python appeared, slithering up the chair and wringing itself around its mistress's shoulders.

Its eerie, slitted eyes fixed Oz with a predator's stare and he looked away. Once again, he wondered why she chose a snake, of all things. Didn't black cats typically give off the 'spellcaster' feeling? Wouldn't it be easier to sell her act with a small, harmless cat instead of a bloody man-eating reptile?

"There was a shadow moon last night," he replied. "I wanted to see what you thought."

"Don't you have a seer closer to ya?" The shuffle resumed.

"Don't pretend like you're not the best, love. It doesn't suit you." He met her gaze once again and she returned a cocky smile to his lopsided one. There were a few other reasons he preferred her practice--chief among them was the selfish notion of comfort he took that the woman was also a foreigner. In Ri'shii's capital city, the skin tone ranged from caramel to shadow black. Even light skinned tourists were rare. Though Oz was not from the Greene Isle like the seer, the fact that she, too, was out of place made him feel a little less like an oddity.

Handing the deck over, Ozwald himself shuffled and cut it. Sliding the right half to the side, he settled back down.

"Aye, I suppose you're right, Che." In a single, smooth motion, the cards were fanned out before his hands, and she said, "Let's see what the cards have to say about this omen."

Picking three cards--one from the left, right and center of the semicircle. Their fingers brushed as the seer moved forward to flip them face up. Oz felt lightning dance across his skin but hid his pounding heart behind a half-smirk. The grin was wiped off his face the second he saw her expression shift.

The Moon, Justice, and The Devil, all upright.

"The Moon," She began to explain "the card of fear, illusion, and intuition. Justice: cause and effect, law, and truth. And The Devil, restriction, attachment, and a shadow self."

"So... what does all that mean? In not-psychic speech, please, love." He asked.

"Secret enemies will have justice, and the one who is wrongly controlled by darkness will be set free." Her olive eyes looked into his, and for a moment he saw something dark cloud her gaze. But it was gone in an instant, and Oz stood up. He had to get back to the boss and double security. Pausing when his hand was on the doorknob, he turned back to call thanks, but found she'd shadowed him. Looking down at the woman, Ozwald took her rough hand, gently, and kissed her knuckles. When he lifted her hand to his lips, a drooping sleeve receded to her elbow, and he caught a glimpse of the small star tattoos that littered her skin, much akin to freckles.     "Thank you so much, love, I know this taxes you." Indeed, she looked notably more drawn than before.

"Bah," She waved him off with a jeweled hand, rings winking and bracelets chiming. "Think nothing of it, Che. Just tip me well at the next appointment."

Halfway out the door, he said, "My darling seer, you're an angel." With an indignant scoff, she replied, "Where I come from, those are called Faeries."

Now farther down the street, he turned, grinning, and called back, "Then you're the Queen of the Faeries!" Oz thought he spied a blush bloom on her pale cheeks and continued his walk back with a little spring in his step, despite the grim warning.

He made a note to ask her about the tattoos next time.

* * *

She closed the shop for the day, sliding the heavy deadbolt into place and sighing. Resting her forehead against the cool wood, the teller began to gather her remaining strength. Oz's hands were so soft. His soul was so new--so young and, despite his shadowy enterprises, not totally corrupt. Though she chided herself, just because his soul was familiar doesn't mean he should get special treatment. She shouldn't even be calling him Che;

references to past lives were strictly forbidden. But since no one else could hear, she couldn't help herself. Her own hands were heavily creased, lines laying atop one another like half-erased sketches. The seer's soul was very old, and heavy with purpose.

"It's time," she murmured to herself, pushing off the door and going towards the back room. Coiled neatly in her now vacant nest chair, Tector's slitted gaze bore into her. "I know, I know." She said, flipping the long braid over her shoulder. "Sleep first." Satisfied, the python slid from the chair and settled close to the fire, forked tongue flicking happily as his body lapped up the warmth. Now in her quarters, the teller shucked off her jewelry, barely collapsing into the hammock before she was stolen away by sleep. Tonight, the real work began.

* * *

A slim silhouette flickered across the moon. Her strides were easy, loping along the slanted slate rooftops with no resistance. Not breaking pace, she leapt nimbly from the edge of one roof to another, unfazed by the plunge each gap promised with a misstep. The night was frigid, the darkness clawing at her legs as she danced in and out of the moonlight. Shadows and luminescence fighting for her like hungry wolves; She belonged to neither-- forever in limbo.

Finally, arriving at the Crow's nest, she pressed herself against the damp roof and Tector unwound himself from her frame. "Be safe, my friend." She whispered, and the snake blinked tenderly back, flicking her nose with his forked tongue. He then slid along the shingles and vanished down the chimney. She waited breathlessly, fingers growing numb as they clung to the cold stone. The glass below her feet rattled gently, and she descended, settling into the windowpane. Sliding a slim metal rod through the gap in the glass, she unhooked the latch and let herself in. Quickly closing the window behind her, there was a thick sucking sound as the cold air was cut off, and the fire spluttered. Three men lay on the floor--two by the glass doors to the terrace and one by the door that leads to the house.

Checking the closest one for a pulse, she sighed in relief when the steady beat thrummed under her fingertips. "Good job, Tector." The snake, who was coiled by the fire, gave the redhead an indignant look. She rolled her eyes, lips turned up, slightly. But her expression hardened again as she approached the bed. An elderly man with hard, coarse features was sleeping soundly under the blankets. Climbing up, she situated herself atop him, knees pinning his hands to the mattress. He began to stir, and she leaned down, murmuring, "Wake." Dark eyes flying open, the man stared up at her, blood draining from his copper face. He didn't struggle or make a sound. "You know who I am?"

He stared up at her, so close he could count every freckle. Her deep olive eyes were cold and hard, braid cascading over her shoulder, lips stained blood red. The mob boss knew without looking that her forearms were decorated with small black stars. Licking his dry lips, he breathed out:

"Soul Eater."

"That's right." Her ageless eyes searched for any sign of remorse, regret, or even fear. She found nothing but greed, lust, and hatred. Placing her rough hands on either side of his face, she began, "You have lost the right to be reborn." The vile man could feel the lines etched into her skin, the stories of a thousand lifetimes, countless rituals like this. Ending the cycle of reincarnation for souls that were beyond repair. Beyond repentance.

"It is my duty to end your blackened spirit. You have tainted the immortal flame within yourself so it can no longer do good to the world. Do you deny my claim?"

For a split second he considered it. But that thought crumbled almost as soon as it was born--an entity who'd lived so long had heard every excuse, every plea. There would be no persuading her. The query was merely procedure--a courtesy, maybe.

"No."

"Then I banish your damned soul to the void. If you ever deserved mercy, I will pray it finds peace." She leaned forward to seal his fate--to add his blood to her lips.

"Wait." She froze, his death only inches from his face. "I have a question." Cocking her head, the Soul Eater looked at him in puzzlement.

"Why would I answer the question of a criminal?"

"I never said you would. I just want to ask." His sharp eyes did not fit the age of his face. She knew how he became so powerful; his mind was far younger than his body. When she didn't object, he continued, "Is it true your soul is so old, it has forgotten its name?" Without replying, she closed the gap between them. His sharp eyes clouded over, and his pulse pounded to a jittery halt. Slowly lifting her face from his, a small, black-blue flame followed her lips.

Cupping it with her hands she swallowed the soul, eyes closed, head tilted back. When the burning sensation died down in her throat, a new star appeared on her left forearm. She hesitated for a heartbeat, staring at the blank ceiling.

* * *

Bursting into the boss's room, Oz saw it truly was too late. "Dammit!" Blood spattered the bedspread--a clean cut to the throat. Whoever did the hit had been quick about it. All three guards had been knocked out without a sound. He stood there in shock, bad leg throbbing from his mad dash up flights of stairs. Who was going to run the gang now? Who could coordinate everything as well as the old man? Running a panicked hand through his dark hair, Ozwald froze as another thought bubbled to the surface.

His debt was nullified.

He was free. He could walk right back down those stairs and out the front door and never look back. Suddenly, he was shoved, slightly, from behind. Snapping out of his thoughts, he looked over his shoulder to find Kit, a gangly, wild haired teenager whose caramel skin was always covered in gunpowder, staring in horror at his grandfather. When the boy began to draw closer, Oz laid a heavy hand on his shoulder. "Don't do that to yourself, kid."

The teen was beginning to shake as Oz drew him back out of the room. He had seen the violence of war--so the man was unfazed. But this was probably the first time Kit had even seen blood--his grandfather had kept the boy holed up in the workshop fixing guns and making bombs. Partly because the kid was a genius, partly because he'd wanted to protect his only surviving family. This boy was now alone. The thought unsettled Ozwald, like he was holding his ghost at arm's length instead. "W-what are we gonna do, now?"

Looking around, Oz saw that other members of the gang were looking towards him for guidance, too. *Am I really gonna stick around?* Thinking for a few moments, he sighed softly. Oz never was good at quitting while he was ahead. What was a crippled vet gonna do in the slums, anyway? Looking back at the teen with his signature crooked grin, he replied, "I'll take care of it."

* * *

The Soul Eater gasped sharply, eyes flying open. From her lap, Tector stirred, lifting his head, and twisting to face her. She'd been meditating before the fire, praying to Fate that the foul man's soul might find peace. It had been a true flame once after all. The seer's prayers had been interrupted by a fragment of Oz clapping a young boy on the shoulder, grinning that scheming smile of his. The last part of her prediction had come through, yet though Ozwald was free of his debts, he remained with the Crows. Tector had wound his way around her shoulders now, flicking his tongue in concern. Shaking her head tiredly, she stroked the smooth scales on his head, warm to the touch thanks to the fire.

"I'll never understand humans. They are given so many chances at life, yet always make the same mistakes." She sighed, and muttered to herself "Mother, please. Don't make me take him too."

### *Horns*

Fire burst from his palm, its flickering light casting a sinister light over his grin. As he alone advanced, the soldiers before him remained stoic, stony faces and hands on their swords, frozen until orders brought them alive. Little tin men waiting for the puppet master. The mage mused, letting his shaggy brown hair cover his amber eyes.

He tossed the fireball over his shoulder, igniting the massive summoning circle behind him. It took up half of the valley, and as the fire greedily grew, so did his wicked smile. When the hissing of flames eating salt died, he snapped his fingers and acid green fire sprung forth. A great tremble shook the earth, knocking many of the tin men flat. The circle split open and two massive, clawed hands gripped the edges, followed by the gigantic body of a demon.

Her skin was ash gray, with hair made of flames and thick spiraled black horns sprouting from her temples. Her black lips peeled back in a twisted smile, exposing sharp fangs. She stretched her bat like wings, showcasing her rippling muscles. Once fully above ground, she roared, throwing her head back like a beast. The mage followed suit howling with her, and when he turned his eyes back to the battle they had a feral glint to them. Taking another deep breath, he called out,

"Orion! You can't hide behind those little toy soldiers forever!" The golems opened their mouths and their master's voice came slithering out as an eerie, metallic echo. "It's better than selling your soul to that woman, Aquila,"

"We'll see about that." As one, the soldiers surged up, charging. To a lesser man, the tide would have seemed unstoppable. Aquila leapt backward with an almost inhuman grace, the demon's gray skinned hand snatching him out of the air. She lifted him up as the army advanced, and he took his place upon her shoulder. Standing, he grabbed onto one of her massive black horns and leaned out, scanning the area. "Now, my lady, would you mind decimating those little toys while I search for their master?"

Unfurling her whip with a crack that birthed thunder, the demon replied, "Gladly." She sent out her whip, and it twirled around her with an unexpected grace, cutting through the golems like butter. As his lady took care of the onslaught, Aquila worked to figure out which vantage point his opponent would be hiding in. He finally zeroed in on a cliff jutting out just before the valley's crumbling castle. It was close enough to be in range for the Golem's magic, but far enough to see most of the battlefield.

"Oh lover," he called, leaning back towards her pointed ear. "I need to get to that cliff there, think you could lend me a hand?"

"Clear a path for me and I can," she replied. "Of course!" he said jovially, as if he'd just agreed to lay his coat over a puddle. She set him down and Aquila dusted himself off. Taking a deep breath, he placed a fist over his mouth, lifted his pinky to create an opening through his fingers. The mage exhaled, torching the ground before him in a torrent of flames. The tin soldiers had been cleared--for the moment. But it was enough. Her powerful legs ended in goat's hooves, and each step was akin to an earthquake. Scooping him up, she moved to the cliff, her whip clearing the Golems from before her and her flaming tail from behind. Depositing Aquila at his destination, she turned and went back to battle. "Many thanks, my lady!" he shouted after her, receiving no response.

There was a whistle in the air behind him and the mage had just a heartbeat to duck as a club came screaming towards him. Spinning on his heel as he crouched, Aquila blasted his attacker with white hot fire, incinerating the Golem.

"So, you do have a brain in that fat head of yours," Orion taunted through another puppet. Punching through said puppet's face, Aquila advanced, sharp amber eyes searching for their master.

"Contrary to what you believe, it does take intelligence to contract such a beauty as my lady," he shot back, continuing to fell Golems as he moved.

"Beauty? Aquila, you are truly mad," Orion replied, summoning another one of his toy soldiers from the earth and sending it forth. Finally, Aquila was within striking distance.

Having bested Orion's last Golem, Aquila launched himself at his opponent with full force. They fell to the ground, grappling as they rolled down the steep hill that led up to the cliff. When the pair came to a stop, they continued to trade blows and curses, until a shadow came over them.

"And you call yourself mages?!" a deep voice boomed in disgust. The men looked up, bruised and bleeding. For once, the expressions on their faces were mirrored, slightly terrified apologetic grimaces. "Up! Now!" They scrambled to their feet, clothes torn and covered in soil. The man before them sighed heavily, pinching the bridge of his nose. "Aquila, send back that thing you called. Orion, clean up your mess."

"Yes, master," they chorused.

"Then return to the castle. I'll think of an appropriate punishment for the two of you there." He turned and started back to the fortress. They squabbled behind his back as they knelt. Orion would draw a circle around himself with his wand and reabsorb the metal he'd borrowed to the earth once more. Aquila would banish that demon he'd chained himself to back to hell. Honestly, the master fumed silently. Mages of their talent, fist fighting of all things-- he sighed again, stopping. Looking towards the moon, still visible in the daytime sky, he shook his head in grief. *Why such a fate for those two boys?* He wondered, asking the gods as he had so many times before. *And why choose me to set them on that path?*

Once they had returned home, he sent them to their rooms. "Your wounds can heal themselves, since you saw the need to inflict them upon each other. Goodnight."

* * *

Though it had barely been sunset when they had been banished to their rooms, Orion still found Aquila fast asleep in his room when he snuck in before dinner. Rolling his eyes, he kicked Aquila in the shin. "Wake up, you lout." He scolded. Aquila jolted awake, looking around in a daze.

"Wha-? Oh, it's just you. Is it dinner time already?" Aquila sat up and rubbed his hands over his face. He regretted his action immediately as his fingers brushed over a cut on his forehead.

"No." Orion replied. "I've smuggled something in for us–here." He tossed a roll of bandages and a tin of salve to him. Aquila caught it and gave him a grin. "Aw, you do care! I'm touched."

"Shut up and sit still, brute." Orion snapped back, dragging a stool from across the room to sit before him. He took the wet cloth he'd stolen and wiped the blood from Aquila's tan face, getting a better look at the damage. "You'll need stitches on your head but the rest should be fine. Hold still." Orion applied the salve to the bruises and cleaned cuts then bandaged what he could. Once he was finished they switched roles. Aquila wiped away the blood on Orion's face.

"What will we do if the old man lets this scar?" He tutted teasingly. "We all know your only redeeming quality is your face."

"Better than having rocks for brains." Orion responded, wincing as the salve stung the scrape on his cheek. "Yes, yes." Aquila said in a placating tone. "Done. Now get out before we're caught." Orion stood and kicked Aquila's leg as he went towards the door causing him to fall back onto the bed.

"I'll get you next time. Just watch."

## *Heartless*

The city beyond him glittered like fallen stars in the snow. The flickering lights carved a warmth into the frigid mountain where the kingdom lay, and Dolon admired it from the highest spire. Even with the cold bluing his fingertips, peace settled over him. Up this high there was a stillness one would not see in the overcrowded capital. Dolon savored the quiet that wrapped around him. He was high enough to imagine he was breathing in stardust.

*Dolon.*

He sighed, running a gloved hand through his messy black curls.

"I know, I know. I didn't come here to sightsee."

*Hurry, then. Your country cannot wait.*

Dolon rolled his eyes and grumbled to himself as he began to rappel down the smooth glass of the tower.

"I don't care 'bout this country. I just want you to move out already."

*Most people would consider my presence a blessing.* She snapped back. He mouthed her words sarcastically, sticking his tongue out to their reflection. When the moonlight hit the polished surface just right--he caught a glimpse of the ghost within him. Almond shaped eyes colored an almost violent pink, the curve of her wide nose and a tight frown forming on full lips. Dolon wasn't sure what Katina Re'ose had looked like while she was alive, he spent too much time in his laboratory to attend the rallies.

She had been a forbidden saint, deemed holy by the people and not the church. A figure to unite the people against their heartless prince and was even more influential in death--she had become a martyr. Even a shut-in like himself heard the protests as the common folk took to the streets after her execution. It had been almost a fortnight and the riots had yet to fully cease.

Dolon had finally reached the window. Carefully, he uncorked the vial of bright green fluid from his pocket and let it drip between the sheets of glass.

"You're sure no one will see us?" He asked, his nervousness creeping in.

*No one.* She confirmed. *As long as I'm here, you're a ghost, too.*

"I didn't need you for that to happen." Dolon muttered.

With a gentle curl of green-tinted smoke, the sealer for the window melted away. Once his elixir had done its work it was all too easy to pry the glass loose, though his fingers were nearly numb.

Grunting as the panel fell into his arms, he wrestled it through the new opening silently.

Once he was inside, Dolon unhooked himself from the tether and started fixing the window back into the pane temporarily.

"Why couldn't I be possessed by Boris the Hammer?" He complained in an annoyed whisper. "Or some Saint that's, you know, actually helpful?"

*Well, I didn't ask to have my spirit stuck inside some half-baked alchemist that's grubbier than a Morelian bog toad! You don't hear me whining!*

"Great Mother," He exclaimed under his breath "How did such a nasty woman become a Saint?" Finishing, he turned around, and scanned the room.

The residents of the palace thought themselves invincible. The only way into the room the tower held was from a fortified port hole in the floor that was guarded around the clock. But the inside of the room itself was empty. It was thought to be impenetrable from the outside. All Dolon had to do was pluck the pulsing heart-shaped jewel off its pedestal and waltz off. After he scaled down the tower's outer surface without being seen by the guards, of course. Walking to the pedestal, he removed the Crown Prince's heart and stowed it safely in a buckled pocket over his own.

*Good.* Katina said, sounding pleased. *Let's get out of here.*

"Hold on." He murmured. Crouching, he took out his dagger and began to carve into the side of the stone.

* * *

Finnly woke with a gasp, clutching his chest. His dark eyes roved the room, searching for what had disturbed him.

"What a most curious sensation..." He muttered into the dark, relaxing enough to remove a hand from his chest to run through his long gold hair. It felt like someone had grabbed his heart. He didn't have time to waste staying up for no reason; there was too much to do tomorrow. Sighing, he lay back down and sank back into sleep.

Dawn broke soon after, and the prince rose to begin the day. As servants helped him dress, his butler, Avi, read the day's schedule aloud. "After breakfast, you have a meeting with the High Priest about the martyrdom of that forbidden saint that was executed a few weeks ago."

The prince sighed. "Just as we predicted." People with hearts were so predictable. Avi nodded in agreement, then continued "Then you have four hours of open court." Finnly ran through the issues they'd discussed last session in his mind quickly. "And after that?"

"Wedding interviews." The prince gave a short nod. He was of age now, it made little sense to put his wedding off any longer. Checking himself over in the mirror one last time, he straightened the cuffs of his suit, sapphire cufflinks glinting. Turning on his heel the crown prince left, Avi in tow. As he passed through the doors, his guard joined them.

"Good morning, your majesty." Enzo rumbled, his deep voice echoing through the empty hall.

"Report on the night patrol?"

"All quiet."

"Excellent. Keep up the good work." Finnly responded. Enzo bowed as Finnly placed his hand on the door to the study.

"Have a good day, your majesty." Enzo said.

"Thank you, Enzo. Avi," The butler straightened "Bring my breakfast here. I want to look over the new affairs of the state before the High Priest gets here."

"Yes sire." Avi scuttled off towards the kitchen. The crown prince settled into his desk and began methodically sorting through the mountain of documents that quarreled for attention. Soon enough the morning had come and gone, and Finnly was still at his desk when the High Priest arrived. Avi's knock sounded through the wooden doors, and he called out.

"The High Priest has arrived, your majesty." Fin stood quickly, smoothing down his suit and coming around to the front of the desk.

"Enter." Avi obeyed, and behind the butler appeared three figures clad from head to toe in gold gilded white. The prince bowed, and his guests bowed back.

"May the Great Mother guide you." They murmured in unison. When the men stood upright, Finnly gestured towards the chairs. The High Priest seated himself, and his two followers stood on either side of him. Fin leaned back against the desk and folded his arms across his chest.

"It's good to see you again." He greeted.

"You as well, Majesty." the holy man replied, "Though I wish it weren't under such distressing circumstances."

"Indeed." Finnly thought about his next words carefully. "This situation was going to be a mess anyway it played out."

"I'm afraid you're right." The old man sighed.

"Well, you know how the masses work." He replied "All these stunts with the roses and boycotting will die down soon enough. That girl was nothing more than a fad."

"But the riots! Isn't there a way you could…" The old man paused, becoming agitated, his beady eyes darting around the room. Anywhere but the prince himself. "Speed up that process?" Fin felt a twinge in his chest. He supposed he would have felt annoyed if his heart was there. "No, Sir, there's nothing I can do. Being heartless gives me indifference, not magic. The church can withstand a few months of lowered attendance. And I know that you have more than enough in your coffers to fix a broken window or two." The high priest opened his mouth to speak again, and Finnly cut him off. There was too much to do for him to be placating the Priest. "Please, you must excuse me, but I have a number of things to attend to before court opens for the day." Taking the hint, he stood. They all bowed, and Avi showed them out.

Sighing heavily, Finnly pressed his palms to his eyes once the doors had closed. "I really can't stand people. Hearts go wrong so easily." Suddenly, a sharp pain shot through him. Fin gasped in surprise, clutching his chest.

"Sire? Sire!" Avi rushed forward. Another stab of pain, and his legs buckled. It felt like someone had caused an avalanche in his chest; his lungs wouldn't take air; his vision became blurry. He had the vague sensation of Avi catching him, then as suddenly as the pain started, it stopped. A strange warmth flooded through him, and Fin gave a small sigh before losing consciousness.

"It's gone!" he was roughly pulled back and Enzo squeezed his way through the small portal. He came around to the front of the altar and swore. Carved and painted on the face were a pair of intertwining roses, one pink and one white. The symbol of the fallen saint.

"I need two more men up here!" he yelled. When they scrambled through, he gave the orders "Look this place over! I want to know how they got in." The guards went to work, and Enzo grimaced. Was this divine retribution? Or the work of rebels?

* * *

Dolon thanked the elderly woman who parceled out the soup for his share. Shuffling over to the camp's fire, he found an empty patch of ground and plopped down, careful not to spill. The caravan of wanderers he'd hitched a ride with were most lively around now, just after dusk. They danced until they couldn't stand, sang until they couldn't speak, and drank themselves to sleep. The next night, they'd do it all over again.

Dolon supposed they needed something to distract them from the monotony of the road. Each night they made themselves a new home around a new hearth, and danced of the joy of it. The young alchemist thought it a testament to their strength. Putting down roots just to tear them up. Dolon himself had been an orphan, stealing and scraping to survive. Seeing them together, a larger family than he could have ever dreamed--it made him ache.

Over the din of the crowd, music began. Cheers rose up, and anyone who could play grabbed their instrument and joined in. People began to dance, pulling each other up and around the fire. As the spirits began to flow, singing started, and soon the nightly merriment was in full swing. Dolon smiled somewhat bitterly, though he was amid the celebrations, he felt wholly detached from it. Slipping out from the main circles, he went to lay down on his bedroll behind the parked wagons.

He pulled off his shoes as he settled down onto the bedding. Pulling his legs to his chest, Dolon raised his eyes up to the stars.

"Am I really doing the right thing?" He murmured into his knees.

*Of course you are!* Katina snapped impatiently. *We're almost to the border. Keep your cowardice in check until then and our country will be saved.* Dolon scoffed, wrapping his arms tighter around his legs.

"It's not the prince's fault his heart was taken away, you know. Maybe if we returned it to him--"

*No.* The saint cut him off. *That man could have put his heart back in whenever he wished after his parents died. Instead, he allies himself with the church and lets his people suffer. Stop thinking like a child.*

*But I am still a child, aren't I?* Dolon thought. He was eighteen, but as Katina's memories began to bleed into his own, he realized how little he really knew about everything. It made him feel helplessly small, and he hated it. Sighing, he crawled into the bedroll and closed his eyes. The sound from the caravan and the light of the stars vanished as he tumbled into sleep. The longer Dolon had Katina, the less like himself he felt. And add on the prince's heart, Dolon felt like he was drowning in foreign memories.

Dolon opened his eyes, recognizing where he was as the room came into focus. It was the crown prince's bedchamber. Looking around, he spotted the blonde-haired boy sitting at his desk. Every night since he'd stolen the heart, Dolon had strange dreams. He dreamt that he was six years old. The prince was there, too and was also a child. He had asked Katina about it, and though she knew little of the magic used on the heart itself, she had guessed that Dolon was being implanted in the memories stored there.

*Don't get attached.* She warned. *It's a distant version of the person he is. And don't interfere with the memories. We don't understand this magic, so we don't know its consequences.*

But watching that young child alone in his room for hours on end, Dolon couldn't stand it. He couldn't watch anyone, let alone any child, be so miserable and isolated. He knew that feeling too well. All night the two would talk and play. Sometimes a young knight would escort the queen in and they would have a stiffly formal conversation. Dolon would have to hide when this happened, as Fin wasn't allowed to have guests.

Tonight, it seemed, he was alone again. Reaching up with a small hand, he grabbed a fistful of the steel blue tunic the older boy was wearing and tugged. "Fin!" He chimed in "Fin! C'mon, let's play!" Finnly turned, looking down at the little intruder. He grinned, then laughed, taking Dolon's hand as he hopped down from the chair.

"Alright Dol, but only for a little while. Mum's coming today."

"Okay!" Dolon smiled brightly, nodding. Fin led Dolon to the center of the room, where there was a large empty space. He then went and brought out his toybox.

"I wanna be the prince today!" Dolon said, snatching up the figure as it spilled out onto the rug. Fin just laughed again, taking up a knight.

"Fine, then. What is your first order, your majesty?" He asked in a silly voice, walking his knight over to the prince.

Dolon laughed. "Send out knights to find all the missing mommies and daddies!" He commanded. Finnly's smile fell, and he stared at Dolon with his clear gray eyes.

"What do you mean, Dol?"

"That's Prince Dol today!" Dolon huffed, puffing out his cheeks.

Fin rolled his eyes. "Okay, okay. What do you mean, Prince Dol?" Dolon made his little prince jump atop a horse and began to trot them around.

"Lots of mummies and daddies go missing." he explained "That's why there are so many of us with Miss Annine." The horse jumped over a few building blocks. "We like Miss Annine a lot, but we still miss our mummies and daddies."

"Dolon…" Finnly's hand came down and rested on Dol's mop of hair, ruffling it. He looked up, and Fin gave him a gentle smile. "When I become king, that's exactly what I'll do."

"Really??" The figures clattered from Dolon's small, dark hands as he launched himself at the prince."Woah--Oomf!" Finnly gasped as he was tackled to the ground. Dolon hugged him as tight as he could, his thank yous falling over each other as they rushed out of his mouth. Tears pricked the corners of his eyes.

"Hey," The prince chuckled, patting his head. "Hey, it's alright. Why are you crying?" Fin sat up, and Dol released him and sat between his legs, unable to stop the tears now.

"B-because," he hiccupped, "if mummy and daddy came back, I won't be alone anymore."

"Dol…" Fin suddenly grabbed the younger boy into a tight hug. "It's okay, Dol. You won't be alone again, got it? You have me." When Finnly pulled away, he gently wiped away Dolon's tears.

Looking over his shoulder, he called, "Katina." The Saint appeared in her human form and sighed heavily. "Looks like the ice prince is a lost soul, too." Dolon said.

She pinched the bridge of her nose. "What do you mean?? Because he made a promise to you, as a child, in a fake dream??" Her face twisted into a scowl. "Children are born pure. This does not prove or atone for anything."

"So, we deny him the potential to be better?" Dolon met her gaze, feeling more like himself than he had in weeks. "Finnly is working with a handicap right now. He's missing something that everyone else has. You were different too. Are you saying you'll crucify someone else like the church did to you?" Katina looked taken aback, shock and rage showing in her face. Before she could interject, he continued. "We don't know what he would do if he had his heart. You're right about that. But what if he does something good? What if he dismantles the church and empties the royal coffers to feed the country? Anything worth doing has risk, right?"

"Damn the Great Mother to hell." She swore.

"Hey, hey! There are children here!" Dolon quickly clapped his hands over the prince's ears.

"Oh, like I care." She snapped, irritated. "Come on, wake up. We better get moving." Dolon stood, the confused prince looking up at them.

"What's going on? Are you really Dol? Who is that?" Finnly asked. Dolon gave a rueful smile and shook his head.

"I'm sorry, Fin, but there's no time to explain. I'll see you soon, though, okay?"

"O-okay..."

Dolon waved and, as soon as he blinked, he was looking up at the still dark sky. He scrambled up and packed his things in a rush. The young alchemist quietly maneuvered through the slumbering camp. An elder sat by the burning coals--all that was left of the fire. She turned to him; her eyes nearly hidden by the wrinkles on her face. But they glinted in the waning moonlight nonetheless.

"Saintspeaker," She said, waving him over "Come, sit with me." Dolon knew that they were pressed for time, but the woman had piqued his interest. He went over and obediently sat beside her.

"Saintspeaker?" He looked at her curiously.

"Yes," She replied, "You who speak for the fallen Saint that guides you. I see her, too." Both Dolon and Katina started, mouths agape. "What? How?"

The elder chuckled. "Wanderers like us don't conform to any church. We have faith in the land, faith in our feet. Souls that are stuck here, we see them. They are like us."

"So do you know how she can, you know, pass on?"

*Rude.* Katina huffed. Dolon rolled his eyes. He waited patiently as the old woman put together her thoughts. The common tongue was somewhat difficult for the older members of the caravan, as they spoke mainly in their mother language. "She must find rest." Dolon placed a hand on her shoulder when she started to speak again. He smiled kindly at her.

"Thank you." She smiled back, relieved that she'd said it right. "I have to ask a favor of you." Dolon said, "I need a horse. I'll give you all I have left, but I must leave before the first light."

She looked into the embers thoughtfully. "What can you trade us for a good horse?" Dolon ran through a silent checklist of everything he had. He only had two things of real value on him: the prince's heart and a scroll containing the formula to his homemade acid potion. The young alchemist was quite proud of it; the liquid would burn through anything but was harmless on flesh. He pressed one hand over the jewel, feeling its pulse merge with his own. Sighing heavily, Dolon took out the scroll case from his bag. He had to look away as he gave it to the elder, a bitter pain shooting through him as he let go of his creation. Dolon sighed. He'd probably never get the combination right again. "That formula works. Show it to any alchemist and you'll make enough to buy ten horses."

"You're in love, aren't you?" She chuckled, taking it.

After a moment, he replied. "Not in the way you're thinking." The elder just smiled and laughed.

"Take a steed, Saintspeaker. And may your travels be safe along the road back." Dolon thanked her and took one of the packhorses. Better not to leave a wagon down an animal. He turned the horse back toward the fire and called, "Thank you!" Spurring the animal on, the teen went galloping off toward the horizon. Dolon fumbled with the reins and slid around in the saddle, struggling to find his balance. But his steed was seasoned and its gate steady. He managed to gain some semblance of stability atop the animal. Until Katina started talking.

*This is completely idiotic.*

"You saw him." Dolon retorted, giving the horse more slack. "It wasn't his choice. We can't take the heart of someone who wasn't given a chance."

*No chance? By the Saints, he was given chances others in the country can barely fathom!*

"I'm not talking about his status!" Dolon snapped, feeling anger begin to itch at his throat "He never had a chance to feel. Never got the choice to have emotions. Don't you see how unfair that is?"

*Unfair? Dolon–*

"He was raised to be the perfect machine. He doesn't know better, he can't fathom what emotions are, how powerful they can be. All his memories of them were locked away." The wind raked back his messy curls, stinging his eyes. Dolon's throat was almost completely closed now, anger moving up to heat his face. "I-I'm not trying to excuse what he's done, okay? Not knowing better isn't a reason to justify anything. The fact is, he can't."

For the first time, Katina's silence filled him with unease. Moments passed with only the whistling wind and the beat of hooves.

*Crouch lower over the horse's neck.* She said in a quiet voice. *And lift off the saddle slightly with its strides, it'll be a smoother ride that way. I'm not saying you're right, just that you make a good point.*

Heeding her advice, Dolon crouched over the saddle and matched his rhythm to the horse's stride.

* * *

"Majesty--"

"Avi, I swear to the Great Mother, I'm fine. If I don't get back, I'll be up to my waist in paperwork." Fin worked to wrestle past his very concerned servant only to be met at the doors of his chambers by the iron wall known as his head guard. Enzo arched a brow in disapproval, arms crossed over his chest.

"Your Majesty." he said, looking down at the two men. "I suggest you listen and take a day of rest."

"Enzo, really, concern is not necessary, as I have already told Avi--" A heavy hand landed on his shoulder, and then the room started to move. Before Finnly could utter a sound, he was slung over the man's shoulder.

"Excuse me!" he spluttered as he was carried across his chambers. With a muffled whump the crown prince was unceremoniously thrown onto his bed. "Enzo, where in the world did you get the nerve to--" but the knight was already back at the door.

"Apologies, Majesty, but I believe it is in your best interest to stay here and rest. Avi will attend to your papers, and I will be right outside should you need anything." The pair bowed and the doors swung shut. Fin blew blonde strands out of his face, leaning back onto his elbows as he stared at the ceiling. It was nearly noon, and he hadn't done a single bit of paperwork. He hadn't had a day like this since…. Well, Finnly couldn't remember. Closing his eyes, he fell back into the bed completely, releasing a sigh. The prince hardly knew what to do with himself, running the Kingdom was his life. Fin was so caught up in his thoughts that he didn't even notice the intruder in his room until a weight landed heavily on his lap. Snapping open his eyes, Finnly only had a momentary look at the face of his attacker before one of the man's brown hands slammed into his chest.

"Sorry Fin, but you'll thank me in a minute!" The world blurred, and Finnly sucked in air with the sensation of his whole body being crushed by a stampede. He was overwhelmed with feeling. His pulse skyrocketed, his hands shook, and his blood rushed through his ears. It was like every nerve on his body was on fire, his brain sending signals for everything he'd never felt all at once. When the overwhelming feeling stopped, he blinked rapidly up at the youth straddling him.

It was a boy around his age with coppered skin and a heap of messy curls framing his thin face. "Fin? Fin, can you hear me? How do you feel?"

"What? Wait--" The prince narrowed his eyes, going over the vagrant's face again. A blurry memory began to surface, and features started to overlap with the one above him. "Dolon?" Something warm spread through his chest when a lopsided grin cracked Dolon's face wide open. "Great Mother… How long has it been? What happened to you?" The smile fell.

"Finnly those were dreams. I think I relived some memories of you before your heart was removed. I know it's been a long time since then, but I still feel like I know you. I still feel like we're friends. And thinking about you, here, without the heart that made you so kind and--"

"Wait…" Fin's eyes widened. Propping himself up on one elbow, his other hand frantically clutched his chest. It felt heavy. He felt heavy. "Dolon," He murmured "What did you do?" He looked up into the other boy's eyes. Dol gave a nervous, almost guilty smile, lowering his gaze.

"I, uh, stole your heart. Literally, I mean." His face flushed "Out of the tower. Katina--that saint the church killed--she made me do it. I'm kind of possessed by her. We were going to give it to the Morelians." Fin stared at him, mouth agape. "N-not for money, of course!" Dolon added hastily "Just as a bargaining chip. To make you…stop."

"Stop? Stop what?"

"Stop screwing over the people." Finnly blinked in disbelief. Dolon still wouldn't meet his eyes.

"Fin, the way you've been running this country its efficient, sure, but the people are suffering. And I… I would know." He gave a sad smile, finally meeting the prince's eyes. The warmth in Fin's chest crumbled and was replaced by a fierce aching.

"Dolon…" Fin whispered. Could it be true? Those memories weren't real? The pain on Dol's face was real enough. The things he felt were very much real too. Reaching out he pulled the other boy down into his chest and hugged him tightly. "I'm so sorry." Dolon returned the embrace, and a strange warmth washed over him. Hesitantly, he laid a hand on Dolon's head, his fingers becoming tangled in the soft curls. He held Dolon as he began to tremble and sob softly. "You don't ever have to be alone again, remember?"

* * *

Katina watched the reunion from the balcony. She heard Dolon begin to cry, and saw Finnly embrace him. "Maybe the kid was right." She said to herself. "I hope he was."

"Time will tell." A calm voice beside her answered. Startled, Katina turned. Another ghost had appeared, a lithe woman with dark brown skin and deep green eyes.

"Who the hell are you?"

The woman laughed, eyes crinkling at the corners. "I used to have a name." She said, "But now I'm just called Mother." Katina turned back to the boys. She watched as the breeze caught the sheer curtains and blew the fabric through her body.

"If you're here to tell me it's time to go, I'm not leaving." A hand landed on her shoulder, solid and warm. Blinking rapidly in surprise, Katina turned her head to look at Mother.

"Hardly. You're still too restless." There was a kindness in Mother's voice that Katina was unaccustomed to. "But we'll all still be here when you've settled down. And besides, those boys need someone with a good head on her shoulders."

"We?" Mother steered Katina around to face the courtyard and she saw nine other ghosts waiting there. Many of them smiled, a few waved. "Hold on. Ten Saints? There are only supposed to be seven, including Mother."

"The church does not give us power. The people do." Mother answered, "You should know that better than anyone." The hand lifted from her shoulder. Mother began to drift away and called back. "Being dead doesn't mean your job is done,

Katina. We'll come back to get you when you're ready."

As the figures vanished, Katina huffed and crossed her arms, again returning her gaze to the living. "Guess I'm stuck with these two for a while."

## *Rage*

Wendy was excited to finally be able to join the sewing circle. She was fourteen now–all grown up and skilled at most things women needed to know. She could cook, clean, and care for livestock and children. All she needed to know now was how to sew, and sew well, before she could become a real adult woman.

Her mother brought her younger sibling to their neighbor's home that afternoon, they would be away until past nightfall and the boys were still in the fields. She and her mother arrived at Mrs. Tanner's house after about a half hour walk through town and were greeted warmly at the door. There was food piled up in the kitchen and Wendy could smell the bread still in the oven. Hints of cinnamon and honey–it was Mrs. Lowell's famous sweet bread! She grinned as they were led into the living room, where women of all ages from down sat in a large circle. The mismatched chairs, the couch, the rug, wherever they could find purchase.

Wendy had known everyone in the room all her life and was eager to finally be accepted into the group for what she felt she was–a grown up. She took a seat on the floor as her mother squeezed into the last spot on the couch. Each woman had her own project, though some took multiple people to complete, like the Stonewall's quilt. Her granddaughter was going to be born soon.

Sometimes things would be passed around for the younger girls to practice on or given to someone who had a certain skill. Wendy herself was going to start by learning how to fix holes in a few pairs of worn trousers for her brothers.

During the first few hours they were there, gossip was exchanged. One of the farmers at the market had upped his price for eggs, a raccoon was bothering the Little family's garden, and it seemed that the eldest Marley boy was trying to secretly court Charlotte Waxer–though they were not as good at hiding it as they thought. After the sweetbread was distributed, the air in the room grew different.

"We have many younger girls here tonight," said Mrs. Tanner thoughtfully. "Should we tell the story?" She looked to the other women in the room as below their elbows all the girls exchanged curious glances.

"Not a bad idea." Replied old Mrs. Stonewall, her hands never idling in their work.

"I can begin." Offered Mrs. Little, who still had her newborn strapped to her chest. Wendy watched her fingers expertly loop and pull the thread through the rough fabric of the overalls on her knee as she began to speak, rocking slightly for the babe. When the other women gave a nod of consent, she continued. "There are some stories that we pass down here, in the spaces for women's work. Stories that you should take heed of carefully." They took a brief pause to give advice to the girls who were still learning before the story began.

"A long time ago, there was a beautiful woman named Helen. She was the princess of a mighty country called Troy. She was so beautiful that there was a contest to decide her husband. A pact was made that once the husband was chosen, no other countries would fight over the decision. The contest went on–all trying to prove they were worthy of her. Finally, Helen chose a winner: the King named Menelaus." Wendy sounded the name out silently with her mouth, feeling the heaviness of the strange word.

"A grand feast was staged to celebrate, but during the party, Helen was kidnapped by a young prince named Paris." The young girls in the room let out a collective gasp. The older women shared a wry smile at their reaction.

"Paris ran back to Troy with his new bride, and in response, a thousand ships set sail to fight for her return. Ten long years of war followed, with each side refusing to surrender. Many soldiers fell, and blood colored the soil of Troy." The baby began to fuss, and Mrs. Tanner took over the story while Mrs. Little left the room to tend to him.

"So weary of death and bloodshed, both Troy itself and the soldiers who fought for her began to resent Helen. The gods, too, hated her, for they lost many beloved warriors of their own in the fighting. Gods are fickle things, you see. It was they who urged Paris to steal Helen away, and who fortified the soldiers' hearts to continue the battles. Yet with all their power, they placed the blame upon her. She was trapped and hopelessly alone inside the castle. Even her handmaidens scorned her openly."

Wendy thought this was unfair. After all, Helen had not asked to go to Troy. Paris had been a sore loser and taken her against her will. She thought for a moment about what it would be like to live so far away from home for so long. It would be lonely, of course. Terribly lonely. But Wendy felt more than that. Sparks of anger welled inside her chest at the thought of being made the center of everyone else's problems. She was glad that she was not beautiful, if the fate of beautiful women was simply to be bickered over like a toy.

"How did the war end?" One of the other girls asked eagerly. Wendy realized that while she was thinking, she had stopped sewing. She looked down at her hands and counted her stitches.

"The soldiers that fought for Helen developed a cunning plan. They built an offering to the gods and left it at the gates of Troy, saying that they had given up and left. The Trojans celebrated and brought the offering inside the walls of the city. However, the offering was hollow, and when night fell, the soldiers burst forth and burnt the city down from the inside. They claimed Helen and set sail for home." The story had taken a long time to tell, and it was time for them to depart. With a candle to light the way home, Wendy carried the sewing in her arms as they walked.

"What did you think of the story, my dear?" Her mother asked.

"It made me angry." She replied, peering over the clothing piled in her arms for rocks in the road.

"Oh? Why is that?"

"It wasn't Helen's fault!" She replied, nearly shouting. "Why should she have to bear all that hate alone? Why didn't the gods fix it? Why didn't the kings stop the fighting? Who really cared about Helen?" Her last question was quiet. Her mother stopped and knelt before her.

"You understood the story quite well, Wendy." Her mother circled her hips and pulled her closer, resting her chin on the clothes. "Nobody really cared for Helen. She became something inhuman to all those around her. A harbinger of death to the Trojans, and a prize to fight for, fer the soldiers. She could rely on no one. As a woman, you must be wary of everyone's intentions. Most people are not what they seem."

"That's not fair." Wendy said. "Why do women have to worry about everyone else?"

"You're right." Her mother agreed. "It's not fair. It's lonely and it makes you angry. But it is the way we must live. The story was also meant to show you that everyone feels these things. All women, from the far past, have felt them too."

Strangely, that was comforting. Wendy thought of all the women who had ever lived, passing down this story and connecting with those who had come before. To be able to understand someone from so long ago…it filled her with a sense of peace. At least someone, somewhere, understood what she was feeling. Her mother released her and picked up the candle, resuming their walk. They began to talk about the food they had eaten and the clothes they had sewn. Wendy tucked her rage for Helen deep inside her heart. She would take it out when she felt helpless and alone, to remind her of everything she learned that night.

## *Dreams of Dragons*

Once upon a time, a lord and lady wished for a child. They prayed to the gods every night, and after many years, were listened to. They were given a child born of an elemental dragon's egg.

She was more radiant than the moon. Soft, kind, and intelligent, She mastered everything placed before her and charmed all around her. They named her Ame, for her voice was as gentle and soothing as the rain. As she grew, so did her beauty. Men and women came from the ends of the earth to see her and fell over each other to court her. She was offered riches beyond imagination, art from names that live now in infamy, crowns, and kingdoms. Ame declined all, unwilling, yet, to leave the adoring arms of her parents.

The men who wished for her grew greedy and violent as time went on, killing each other to thin the competition. One night a suitor went so far as to murder her parents so she would be forced to choose a husband. Horrified, Ame was smuggled away in the night by a handful of servants. The emperor, grieved by the tragedy, gave her shelter in his hidden castle, deep in the woods. There the princess grieved, withdrawing into herself. She cursed the gods for her beauty, which drove mortals to much terrible madness. She begged to be turned to a hag, but they refused.

Saddened by Ame's pain, they sent her a companion. A young boy, blinded by an accident and turned away from his home, wandered through the forest. Starved and near death, he collapsed at the gates of the castle. Ame took him in and helped nurse him back to health, though she feared the day he opened his eyes. Finally after weeks of sleeping the boy, Kai, woke. Ame spoke to him from behind a screen, welcoming him into her home. He thanked her and humbly asked for work to repay her, despite his blindness. The princess had never been so overjoyed.

Years passed slowly and the two were never apart. The peace was not to last. The Wind is a chaotic and intense being, sweet and lovely one moment but fierce and destructive the next. As such, lovers are few and far between, for no one can weather his extremes for long. Whispers from the trees told him of an unimaginable beauty living deep within the woods. Curious, he went to see for himself.

He found Ame by a river, singing along to its ethereal music. Her long dark hair fell over her shoulders, loose lavender kimono pooled around her, shimmering in the sunlight. Entranced, he approached her, though he retreated again once Kai appeared. The two smiled at each other as he played along on his flute. Hot jealousy poured through The Wind, and he formulated a plan.

With a strong gust, he blew the willowy boy into the river and he was pulled along by the current. Ame cried out, quickly shedding her outer layer to dive in after him. Suddenly, a whirlpool appeared as the wind blew the river dry beneath Kai's feet. Taking his human form, he swept the boy up into a gentle gust and placed him down beside Ame. The woman wrapped him up in an embrace and wept for joy.

Ame asked how she could repay such kindness, for he had saved the most precious person to her. The wind smiled and asked for a place to stay. Of course, they granted his request and treated him as a most honorable guest. Days passed into months and the wind was persistent in his pursuit of Ame. Despite her growing discomfort, she continued to host him. As time wore on and his beguiling got him nowhere, he began to take out his anger on Kai. It started small, just moving stones for him to trip and branches whacking at his head. It escalated into slamming his fingers in door frames and then shoving him to the ground at any opportunity. Once, Ame caught him and he flew into a blind rage, destroying half the castle in his anger. He changed into the form of a dragon, abducted Ame and flew away with her.

Kai was at a loss, unable to chase after her. He fell to his knees and wept, his tears trickling down to join the river as it swept past. A deep rumbling swelled beneath him, like a thousand rapids thundering in his ears. The river rose from its banks, forming into a watery dragon itself. The great beast blinked slowly, still heavy from slumber. The river asked who placed such bitter feelings into his heart, and Kai relayed his story in a shaking voice. The river sighed deeply, sprinkling Kai with raindrops as he shook his head. How long he had slept, and yet his brother remained the same.

The river bade Kai to stay by the bank for five days and five nights, to play his flute and think of his beloved and his wish for her safety. Without another word, he rushed away, leaving the riverbed dry as he left. Kai had nothing to do but what he was told. His music ranged from bittersweet with longing to bursting with joy as he poured his feelings for Ame into the sound. After five long days and five cold nights, he heard the rushing of the river once more. The sound was accompanied by the clatter of stones and the smell of burning sulfur.

The river spoke, bidding Kai to climb upon his brother, the mountain. With some aid, he did so, and held on tight as they flew above the trees and into the frigid wind. The last brother, fire, told Kai that his music had shown the depth of his love for Ame and that they would save her from the wind in his stead. He would have to promise to play for them as long as he lived. Without hesitation, Kai agreed, only begging that Ame be unharmed.

They arrived at the home of the wind; a grand castle built upon the low hanging clouds. The dragons left Kai upon a small cloud and began their battle. Kai could only listen. It was strangely beautiful for a battle. Their long, graceful forms twined around each other as their elements clashed together. The fight lasted twelve days and twelve nights, the humans waiting with bated breath. Finally, the three came out victorious, having subdued the wind. They swore an oath that the couple would remain untouched by dragons, so long as Ame remained kind and Kai played his music.

## *Five Tails*

Rinkami lay on her futon in a still, quiet temple room. The screen was open, letting the cool rainy air trickle in. The young girl's breathing was rapid, and her face flushed. A monk sat beside her; legs folded under him. He changed the washcloth on her forehead and a small sigh escaped her lips as the cold water touched her skin. He sat back up and returned his gaze to the thin man sitting against the open door.

He was clad in a pale blue kimono etched with stitching of a mountain range. His long silver hair was loosely tied and hung down his back. He was barefoot, and one hand rested inside the front of his montsuki. His sharp, animalistic eyes gazed out onto the courtyard as he fanned himself absently. Without looking behind, he spoke.

"Do you think we're a monster?" The monk looked up, startled. It was the first time the other man had spoken.

He considered the question. "The greatest impurity is ignorance." He replied, "I cannot judge you all, because I know so little." The other man's mouth twitched in a slight smile, exposing his pointed canines.

"That is true. Though I've always hated how humans hide behind the words of their gods." The monk's lips curled in an uneasy smile. "Why have you all appeared, anyway?" Nori's smile faded, looking upon the child that slept fitfully between them.

"She's in real trouble." He replied, "This sickness is strong; its talons have sunken deep into her." He looked back out to the courtyard, where two other figures shifted in and out of sight within the fog. The harsh sound of blades clashing rang out from between the trees. A man emerged; katana drawn. His long hair was tied up in a ponytail, an ash gray color flowing down into ink black. He was soaked through, his light blue robe stuck to his hakama like a second skin. As he backed away from the foliage, a shadow moved. Suddenly, the samurai was on his back, a black clad ninja standing over him. Their swords met again, and the lithe woman let out a guttural growl. The samurai heaved upwards, and the ninja vanished again, the man tailing her back into the trees. "It'll be easier for her body to heal without all of us tumbling around in her brain."

"You mean…?" The monk looked down at the young girl incredulously, and the white fox that was curled tightly at her feet. "Are you all...possessing this child?" The man laughed, a harsh barking sound.

"Still so ignorant, after all this time." Once he had calmed, his other hand emerged from the folds of his kimono and gently rested on the girl's head. "Yes, I suppose that is the best way for you to understand it. She is us and so are we." His gentle smile was somewhat sad as he looked at her. "She has four lifetime's worth of knowledge within her; but that comes with four lifetime's worth of pain. Her body might not be able to handle it."

The monk sat in thought for a moment, then reached out to change the towel on her forehead again. "It is a greater task conquering oneself, than conquering others." The other man laughed dryly and sat back again.

"How true that is."

* * *

Shida found humans more like nuisances than anything. They were loud, messy, and fearful of everything they did not completely understand. Being one of the elder spirits of the forest, she oversaw keeping the peace between humans and spirits. It was harder than she'd expected it to be, at first, but she found ways to appease most. Shida kept the malevolent spirits who required flesh to feed within the borders of the mountain forest, led wayward humans back onto the footpaths if they strayed too far, and was a mediator for every problem in between. Thanks to her efforts, peace had lasted between the two groups for almost a century. Long enough for new generations of human offspring to grow to adulthood.

The new leaders of the village were coming to speak with her. To make demands, really. They laid down the conditions for yokai to be permitted into their village, which areas of the forest they could hunt and gather in, which yokai would be allowed to be near them, which days they were not and the likes. It was, after all, a symbiotic relationship. Many yokai needed the energy and belief of humans to survive and provided services in exchange. Shida expected it to be no different than any other meeting she'd had with humans so far. They would be on edge, trying to seem aggressive to cover their fear. Her ear twitched as she heard footfalls at the edge of the forest. Many footfalls. It seemed these leaders were especially afraid if they brought so many with them.

Shida gave a small sigh before entering the clearing where they were to meet and taking her place on a flat stone by the small pond. A family of Kappas looked up at her from below the water, and she gave an encouraging smile. Wrapping her fluffy tail around her paws, she waited patiently, listening to both the movement of the human party and the rustling of the forest as other spirits gathered within the trees to watch. Finally, the bushes parted and ten–twenty humans filed into the clearing. Three men stepped to the front of the group and gave her a deep bow, which she returned.

"Greetings, o wise one." The first said, straightening. "It is an honor to be in the presence of the white fox who guards the mountain."

"And it is my honor to welcome you to the forest." She replied, lifting her own head. Shida's yellow-gold eyes scanned the crowd of humans, taking note of the weapons they carried in plain sight. "Do you feel unsafe here?" She asked. "Was the forest unwelcoming to you?"

The man gave a small laugh, shaking his head. "No, great guardian. The road outside has become dangerous. We took precautions so as not to be ambushed on our way here." Her eyes narrowed slightly. She had not seen an increase of bandits on the road. Besides, would it not be prudent, then, to leave the warriors at the village, should it be attacked while they were away? She scanned the crowd again, her whiskers twitching at the tension in their bodies.

"What are your conditions this time?" Shida continued, wary. Something was not right. The men smiled at her, their eyes glinting.

"We want the forest." The second leader stated bluntly. "We are tired of having to acquiesce to the will of monsters."

"What?" Shida snarled, pulling her lips back to expose all her teeth. Her ears flattened against her head, her haunches beginning to bristle. "This agreement has been in place for almost a hundred years. We spirits have never broken a single rule you have laid out. How dare you come and demand our home!"

"Yokai are getting weaker as humans grow stronger." The third leader said in a pleasant tone.

"No longer will we deal with you. We will take this forest by force if necessary." Shida felt a rage pulse in every fiber of her being. These arrogant mortals! To be so greedy and ungrateful for all the spirits had provided for them, for their ancestors! Shida's body grew as her rage increased, until she was the size of an elephant.

"Fools! You start a war you cannot comprehend!" She roared, slashing at one of the leaders. The man screamed as his body was thrown full force into a tree. She heard his spine snap on impact and the thud of his limp body crashing onto the ground. The humans dispersed with a collective battle cry, some vanishing into the trees, others trying to rush her. They jabbed at her with spears, slashed at her with swords and daggers.

The screams from the forest distracted her– her heart racing as she heard the spirits fighting and dying around her. She could not protect them all. Shida released a scream of her own, the anguished sound shaking the forest to its very roots. Her eyes glowed golden as she summoned foxfire to rain upon them, the globs of pink and purple flames attaching to the humans, burning through their flesh in moments. They assaulted her still, ignoring the few bodies she crushed beneath her massive paws or limbs she tore with her teeth. Her white fur was pink with blood, a mixture of her own and theirs.

Shida slammed her paw into the body of the first leader, pinning him to the ground but not killing him. "Why?!" She snarled. "Why would you bring death to our people and yours?! For greed?" The man wheezed beneath her, the weight of her slowly crushing his ribcage.

"We will no longer be meek against you monsters!" He cried. Talking was useless. She snapped his bones beneath her foot and went back to defending herself. She needed to kill those closest to her quickly so she could dispose of the interlopers within the forest itself. She needed to minimize the deaths of the spirits in her protection. It took a day and a half to kill them all. By that time, so many had been slaughtered, she had lost count of the bodies of her people. They had attacked the weak, the young spirits who had not matured. She sat beside older spirits as they died of their wounds. In such a short time, the humans had made it deep into the forest.

Shida found she had little care for the malevolent spirits who gleefully fled the trees. She was tired and wounded. Slowly, she began to bury the spirits who left behind bodies. That itself took another day. Shida bid the spirits that would leave to flee to the mountain. The goddess of the region slept there and even the cruelest humans would not dare to invoke her wrath. There were some that wished to stay and take the fight to the humans. The forest did not forget. The malice they wrought would live here for centuries.

Shida returned to the clearing, carrying the bodies of the humans in her jaws. She had to make two trips but deposited them outside the forest in a pile. She would begrudge no one proper burial, even traitors such as these. Death was sacred, no matter what brought it. The pond in the clearing was red with blood, the kappas that had lived there gone. Her body shrunk once more, and she collapsed into a fitful sleep.

When she woke, an elderly human stood over her. He wore the robes of a priest, leaning heavily on a cane. Tears dripped from his hooded eyes, nearly hidden from the wrinkles sagging on his face.

"You killed my only son." He cried, anger and pain clawing out of his throat along with the sobs. "Your son massacred those who had not wronged him." Shida replied, her own voice raw from emotion. "He was a greedy fool."

"He was my son!" The man repeated, glaring at her with hate.

"That does not change his sins!" She snapped back, venom in her tone. "All the death that comes from this is his fault!"

"You took him from me!" The man cried again. Obviously, he was incoherent. Nothing she said would appease him.

"I returned him to you, didn't I?" Shida growled. "He did not show such kindness to my spirits." The man threw down a talisman, which crackled and glowed as energy was released from it.

"I curse you!" He screamed hoarsely. "I curse you to live again until you understand what you have done!" Shida felt tendrils of magic wrap around her, burying itself into her soul. She hissed as the foreign magic mixed with her own. He must be quite powerful to make a spell that could affect her. Her weakened state made her just susceptible to it. As the magic faded, the man fell to his knees and wept. Shida quickly fled the clearing on unstable legs. What would this curse entail? Was there a way to lift it? The goddess would not wake for some time, so her knowledge was inaccessible. Many elder spirits were fighting. Shida would just have to discover what it meant on her own.

* * *

Himiko lay in bed, staring up at the ceiling in the dark. With Oda raging across the continent uniting clans left and right, she was jittery. All the pressure of her clan's worries felt suffocating. Sometimes she wished she got the chance to be normal. But with her name and the strange, wild magic inside of her there was no chance of that. She was only nineteen and already was the best ninja her clan possessed.

Himiko had a feeling she knew what the meeting was about tomorrow, and why everyone had been so jumpy around her. She sat up in bed, her long black hair cascading over her shoulders. She gripped the bedframe hard, before closing her eyes and reaching within herself.

"Are you there?" She asked in a whisper.

*You know the answer to that, child.* A voice responded back, speaking within her own mind. It was not her voice. It was older, deeper. It was comforting to hear that other voice respond. After all, it had always been part of her. This second soul, as she called it, was named Shida. It took the form of a Kitsune and was what helped her become so skilled. Being able to use the talents and instincts of a powerful spirit gave her an inhuman advantage.

When she was old enough, Shida explained her own story. She had once been a powerful guardian spirit but was betrayed by humans. For defending herself and her home, she was cursed. The curse, it seemed, was to be conscious for her next life. Until she understood what she had done. Neither Himiko nor Shida really knew what that meant, taking the life of a child? Everyone was someone's child. Both as a ninja and a fox they understood that. Understood the weight carried once a life was taken. But, Himiko supposed, a curse made in grief could only really be understood by the grieving.

*You should be sleeping, child.* Shida chided. *Young bodies need rest.*

"I'm trying." Himiko responded. "But I…. I'm afraid. I think this life is about to be cut very short." Her heart squeezed at the words.

*I fear you are right.* Shida said. *I am sorry, child.*

"There's no reason for you to be sorry." Himiko shook her head.

*If you did not have my powers, perhaps you would not be chosen.*

"I would go anyway."

*You are a brave and loyal human.* Shida said gently, sadness tinging her voice. *Lay back down, child.* Himiko did as instructed, and listened as Shida began to sing a lullaby in that strange language of yokai.

Himiko was woken early in the morning. Dawn was just breaking over the mountains to the east. Her handmaidens helped her bathe, dress and eat. She was called to the main room soon after her meal was finished and made her way along the polished wooden hallways silently. Staff bowed as they moved out of her way. She knelt by the screen door and announced herself. Her father gave permission to enter, and she did so, taking her seat at his right hand. All the elders of the clan were gathered, looking up at her with stoic expressions. She felt goosebumps rise on her arms.

"Himiko," Her father began, looking at her earnestly. "I must ask something of you, my daughter. I wish I didn't need to, as it is a difficult, dangerous task. But only you can do it." She braced herself to hear the words. "We need you to assassinate Oda." Everyone in the room looked at her with a mix of pity and pride. She bowed her head to the floor behind her hands.

"Of course, father. I will do as ordered." She really was their only chance. Their clan served under a lord that opposed Oda; if he was defeated, they would be wiped out along with him. "I will begin preparations immediately. Where is the last known location of his camp?" They brought out a map and showed her. Taking time to memorize the location, she then left to get ready. Her handmaids had packed her bag of supplies, had her weapons sharpened and laid out her uniform. She sat at the mirror and closed her eyes as they cut her hair to just above her shoulders and then put it up. Himiko let them dress her one last time and left her home without bidding a single soul goodbye. She said nothing to those in the village either. She could not stand that look in their eyes. How they could already see her empty coffin.

"Are you ready?" She asked, once within the forest alone.

*I am.* Shida replied. Himiko took a deep breath, closing her eyes and saying a prayer before allowing Shida's energy to mix with hers. Her senses became sharper–she could hear the flapping of a bird's wings above her head and the skittering of a mouse beneath the foliage by her feet. She could smell the richness of the earth and the growing crops in the fields just outside the village border. Opening her eyes, the colors of the world seemed more vivid, her sight more in focus. Exhaling, her tongue grazed across the pointed teeth. Himiko broke into a run, letting out a small laugh as exhilaration from the simple action filled her body. The wild inside her was freeing.

She found her horse tied up a half mile away from the village, no markings on his saddle or bridle. Swinging up to mount him, she pets his strong neck gently.

"Hello, my old friend." She said, smiling as he tossed his head in response.

*He's excited to ride with you.* Shida supplied. As an animal spirit, she could understand them. Spurring him forward, Himiko began her ride. As they had quite a way to travel, she began to think about the first time she'd merged with Shida. Himiko was just a child, only in her sixth summer. She preferred to roughhouse with the boys and was still young enough that her mother was lenient with her enough to do so. She had followed the boys into the forest in a game of tag, all weaving through the trees and squealing in delight.

Himiko heard a scream, which was cut short. She ran towards the sound, finding a scrawny man with a pinched, mean face holding a knife to one of her friends. His grin was slimy and terrifying.

"Don't make a sound." He warned. She nodded quickly, eyes flicking from the boy to the man. "You're gonna take me into the village and show me the storehouse, got it?" A few other boys had arrived by then, all frozen at the sight of the blade. Her heart was pounding wildly in her chest, trying to figure some way to get him away. Suddenly, she felt a strange tingling all along her body, like lightning under her skin. Himiko was no longer in control of herself; she moved with an inhuman speed, rushing forward, and lunging for him. The only thought on her mind was to protect. She opened her jaws and bit down on his calf with all her strength.

The man screamed in pain, twisting his knife away from the boy in shock. He ran, the other children following suit back in the direction of the village. The coppery taste of blood exploding on her tongue was familiar. Himiko let out a snarl, banging on his leg with her small fists, still locked onto him. He yowled, hopping around as he tried to shake her off. She managed to hold on for quite some time, but he did eventually throw her off. As her body slid across the dirt, she could hear commotion coming towards them. She had bought enough time for the boys to retrieve people from the village. Looking up at the man, she gave him a bloody smile, pointed teeth poking at her lips.

Himiko traveled half a day without rest to reach Oda's camp. She stopped before her horse's hooves could be heard by those patrolling. She climbed down and untacked him, hiding the equipment in the bushes. Petting his long, velvet nose she spoke softly.

"Tell him thank you for everything. Tell him he can return to the village or run free." She pressed her forehead to him as Shida spoke. The horse seemed to shake his head, stamping his foot at her. She gave a quiet laugh. "Tell him he has to go, now." Shida spoke again, and with great reluctance, the steed turned, only looking back once before galloping off. Himiko circled the base several times before finding a vantage point in the trees to observe it. As she waited for nightfall, she took note of the guard rotation and the movements within the camp. She identified Oda's tent, looking for openings. It seemed the only time she would be able to slip in was during the shift change. Himiko ate one meal and left her bag in the tree when the guards began to move. She moved between shadows, her feet not making a sound. Once the guards were far enough away, she managed to slip into the tent unnoticed. She hunkered down behind a large crate which was being used as some sort of table.

With Shida's eyes, there was no wait to adjust to the darkness. Himiko scanned the tent, taking note of where weapons lay, as well as objects that could be used against her. She settled down to wait. All her senses were on high alert as the hours passed, the sensitively almost painful. Hearing every footstep and conversation as they moved past the tent, waiting for the target. It was well past midnight when Oda entered. Himiko adjusted her grip on her dagger, waiting for him to climb onto his bed mat. After another fifteen minutes of shuffling around, Oda did finally lay down, pulling the blanket up over himself.

Himiko quietly began to move after she heard his breathing even out. Tiptoeing over rugs and equipment strewn about she approached the bed, raising her dagger above her head to strike. Suddenly, his eyes opened, and she could barely register the red glow within them before his arm shot out and his massive hand gripped her neck and began to squeeze.

* * *

The temple was quiet in the winter. Nori much preferred the snow-covered stillness to the bustling crowd in spring. Humans were so annoying, yapping and praying and begging the gods to do something for them. As the Kitsune messenger of this temple, He had to take every single prayer and complaint up to the gods. Every. One. They almost never answered. The gods were worse than humans by far, sitting in heaven feasting and partying without care for the mortals who worshiped them. Nori would pity the humans if they weren't so irritating.

He deftly leapt from statue to statue in the garden, leaving sandals footprints on the snow laying atop their heads. His white hair came all the way down to his waist when it was down, though he wore it in a ponytail most days. His large fox ears twitched as they listened to the monks pray inside and the birds pecking at the icy ground around him. He wore a simple montsuki, black and embroidered with pictures of the mountains against the night sky.

*Just go inside if you want to get out of the snow.* A young girl's voice chimed within his mind. Nori let out an irritated tch sound, ignoring her. Having a human inside his head was far worse than having the temple crowded with them. She never left. As the thrice cursed life, he always had two women inside his head, which quickly became a tiring commentary on everything he did. His three tails swished out behind him in annoyance. He let out a sneeze as a large snowflake landed on his sensitive nose. *Fine.* Said Himiko in a snarky tone. *Stay out here and catch a cold. But don't complain that we didn't warn you.*

"Kitsune don't catch colds!" He grumbled, his ears pressing back against his head briefly in his displeasure. Before the argument could continue, he heard a yelp in the direction of the temple stairs. They were closed today on account of the heavy snow. Alighting on the ground, he moved quickly to the staircase leading down to the town, seeing a woman clutching a bundle to her chest splayed out on the stone steps, her knees scraped. "Idiot." he muttered, before moving down the stairs to her. "Can you stand?" He asked, making himself visible to the human eye. The woman looked up at him, a slight tremble to her lips.

"I-I can't. I'm sorry." She was obviously weak, and tears began to bubble in her eyes. Nori had to restrain himself from rolling his own.

"None of that. Hold on." He picked her up easily, holding her to his chest securely as he walked back up the stairs. Marching through the temple yard, he had to kick the front door open and call out. "Someone get Yuki! I have an injured pilgrim!" There was commotion at his words, monks running around as he walked her to the infirmary. The monks were used to his human form and knew what he was though visitors could not see him unless he wished for it. Laying her down on one of the futons, he turned to leave. He stopped when there was a tug on his sleeve. Looking back, he found the woman watching him with a pleading look.

"Thank you so much. Please, can you help my baby?" Nori took the infant as it was handed to him, intending to hand him over to the healer, but stopped. The child was cold, and blue in the lips. Medicine was not going to save him. He groaned inwardly. Humans were too fragile. Moving to the fire on the opposite side of the room, he quickly transformed into his fox form, and curled tightly around the baby. Nori would have to infuse the child with his own life force.

*Who hates humans again?* Teased the voice of Shida. Withholding a growl, Nori responded in his thoughts.

*I'm the temple's guardian. I can't just let a child die. He couldn't imagine the fallout he would have with the gods if he allowed a child to die on their sacred ground.* Curling tighter around the child, he ignored the laughter echoing inside his skull.

The child did survive the night and grew to be one of his biggest annoyances. His name was Yoko, and he visited the temple several times a week. Not to give offerings or pray, but to bother Nori. At eight, he roped Nori into helping him practice archery. At twelve, it was help with swordplay. Fifteen, it was cooking. Every year, some new thing he needed help with. Nori wondered how on earth he was able to hold down an apprenticeship or have time to tend the fields with how often Yoko was following behind him.

This, of course, led to the whole community finding out about him and asking for his help with their issues. Yoko seemed pleased at Nori's recognition, though Nori himself was far from it. At twenty, Yoko became a monk at the temple. After his induction ceremony, they sat together overlooking the garden, drinking some saki that Nori had smuggled in.

"Why did you choose this?" Nori asked "Over everything else you could have done with your life? Humans have a wealth of choices after all."

Yoko laughed, his newly shaved head shaking. "Because I wanted to. That's the beauty of choice, after all."

Nori snorted into his cup before drinking, then pouring himself another. "You mortals baffle me. You have such a finite time to live, and you choose to sequester yourselves here, begging for attention from gods who aren't listening." Yoko grew quiet, sipping on his cup gently. "You never seemed all that devoted to me, anyway." Nori added.

"You're right. I'm not really that devout." Nori looked at him in confusion.

"Then why the hell are you here?? You could have apprenticed with a merchant and traveled the world! Or a blacksmith who made swords and armor!" Yoko downed his saki and placed the cup down. He turned to face Nori more fully, a dark blush covering his face. "Hello??" Nori prodded, before reaching his hand out to try and take his temperature. "Are you drunk already? We haven't even gone through half the bottle." Yoko caught his hand before it could reach him, then turned his palm up and placed a single, light kiss to the flesh there. Nori felt a shockwave run through his body at the contact and he jumped slightly, his golden eyes wide. Yoko gave a nervous smile.

"Because I love you, Nori. This was the only way I could think of being with you." Nori's mouth opened and closed silently, like a carp dragged up from the river. A great burst of laughter broke out in his head.

*I told you!!* Himiko cheered. *I told you, but you didn't listen! Noooo, a silly mortal couldn't possibly LOVE me! HA!*

*Very amusing.* Shida agreed. *I have heard of humans falling for Kitsune, but it was normally due to the fox's seduction. This is certainly new.*

Nori sat frozen, unable to think straight with the voices echoing in his head. He wished he was drunker.

".... Nori?" Yoko asked, still holding his hand, and now looking scared.

*Oh, for the love of the gods! He felt his body tingle and was too dazed to fight it off. He felt an impulse rise inside of him, reaching up to gently grab Yoko's face and leaning forward to kiss him.* When they pulled away, Nori realized she had released him halfway through. A blush of his own set his face aflame as he hurriedly pulled away. Why had he done that?

"Nori." Yoko's voice called him, and he turned back. Yoko's smile was brighter than the moonlight above them. He took Nori's hand in his. "Please, let me spend the rest of my life loving you."

"I'll live much longer than you will!" Nori protested. "You won't find me in the afterlife, no matter how long you wait."

"I know." Yoko said gently, still smiling. "I don't care."

"Why?" Nori spluttered. Yoko laughed at this, a light breathy giggle.

"Because I love you." He replied.

"Why!" Nori repeated. Yoko laughed again, louder this time.

"Because of who you are. You are kind, gentle, sarcastic, and moody. You can't say no to anyone who needs help. Because you were earnest in everything you taught me, even when you didn't want to." Nori felt like the world had turned upside down. Everything Yoko said made no sense to him, but made his heartbeat erratically and made him so, so happy. What was wrong with him?!

*He's so dense he can't even bring himself to think about it.* Himiko mused.

*He's a stubborn one.* Shinda agreed. Had he really been in love with Yoko too? How? When? For how long? He struggled to think back, sifting through his memories as quickly as he could. Slowly, he could see it. Within the last year, teaching Yoko had not been a nuisance. He had enjoyed spending time with him. Nori had gone out of his way to personally oversee his trial period with the monks. His face reddened further; his ears pasted to his head in embarrassment.

"I'm an idiot." He groaned, covering his face with his clawed hands. How had he let himself fall in love with a human? And then been so blind to it?

*You're an idiot.* The girls agreed. Yoko laughed, wrapping the taller man into a tight hug.

"You're my idiot." he said, teasingly.

The years passed quickly after that. Nori and Yoko ran a daycare of sorts within the temple, watching the village's children so the mothers could work. They helped by teach anything and everything they could. Yoko seemed to glow the older he got, bringing happiness to everyone he touched. Nori eventually told him about the curse, which was why he would not meet him in the afterlife. Instead of being appalled, as he thought, Yoko wished to know more. He spent time listening to the stories of his past lives, and even searched the temple's texts and talked to wandering priests about breaking curses.

In the blink of an eye, Yoko stood beside Nori, short and gnarled. His handsome face weathered by time and leathery from his work in the temple garden. They saw the last of the children back to their mothers as the temple closed. Yoko sighed and leaned into Nori, who helped him back to his room to rest.

"You should let me watch them alone some days." Nori scolded, gently laying him down on the futon. Yoko laughed dryly; his voice now almost unrecognizable.

"Nonsense. You'd be lost without me. They'd overtake you." Nori softened.

"That's true," he conceded. "Shall I get dinner for you?"

"No." Yoko shook his head, then waved away the worried look on his lover's face. "I'm just tired. I'll have dinner later."

*I smell death on him, little fox.* Shida warned gently. Nori knew that. Yoko had smelled of death for the past few weeks. Nori could only watch as he grew weaker. He knew the time was near. Gripping

Yoko's thin hand, he raised it up and placed a kiss on his knuckles.

"Alright, my dear. Sleep." He felt tears bubbling up in his eyes as Yoko closed his own, and Nori began to sing. It was an old song, one he never had to learn. In his mind, Himiko and Shida joined him, gently singing beside him. For once, he was grateful for them. He didn't feel so alone as he watched Yoko slip away to a place he could not follow.

The funeral was held some days later. The crowd was so massive that the temple could not hold them all. For a week after the burial, people came to cry and pray. Nori found it comforting. To see how beloved Yoko was, how missed he was. He would live on in the memory of the town. Finally, the grave was quiet. Nori transformed into a fox, just as he had done the day they met. He curled up into a ball on Yoko's grave. It had been snowing for two days and he made a nest within the fresh powder there.

*Are you sure?* Shida asked.

*I'm tired.* He replied. *And empty. Let me sleep.*

*Alright, Nori.* Himiko said quietly. They stopped speaking. He let the snow cover him.

* * *

It was a marriage of convenience. Kauru knew that. His bride did too. He watched her as they sat through the ceremony, and her face was a measured expression of nothing. At least he knew she felt the same way. The ceremony finished and the banquet began, their fathers both looking proud. It was long and tedious. They both had to pretend to be thrilled as everyone greeted them and asked questions. When it was over, they were escorted to the bridal chamber. They met on the futon after bathing, and he finally got a good look at her without the trimmings and makeup. She was pretty. Her eyes were cast downward, and her hands were folded into her lap, waiting for him to speak.

"I know you have no affection for me, Minori." He said gently. She gave a twitch and replied. "I'm sure I will grow to, my lord." He shook his head.

"I do not expect that from you. I will make sure you are comfortable and free to do as you like as the new lady of the Ito family. I will not touch you if you do not wish for it."

She looked up at him, startled. "What? What about an heir?"

He shook his head again. "I don't care about an heir, though don't tell my father that." She continued to look at him incredulously. He shrugged. "You are here now, Minori. It is my duty to care for you. If a child comes to be, so be it. If not, then that is how it is." He was sure his brothers would have children. He could always name one of them his heir. Thinking the conversation over, he turned to begin getting into bed. She stopped him.

"Then lay with me tonight, my lord."

"Are you sure? Do not let the words of outsiders pressure you. As your husband, I will not lay with you for them." She shook her head.

"It is my duty as a wife, my lord. We should at least try for a child."

"Alright. If that is what you wish."

After they lay together, and she fell asleep, he pulled on his robe and left the room. He hurried along the corridor and found an empty guest room, quickly shutting the door behind him. He slid down onto the floor, panting and grabbing at his hair desperately.

That thing inside of him was trying to get out. It made his skin prickle, like energy within him was bursting through his veins. He could hear the beginnings of voices in his mind, sentences starting and stopping as he shut them out. He struggled with all his might to shove the feeling down inside himself, to force it back into dormancy. All his life, he'd had episodes like this. He thought he was going crazy when he was young, hearing voices overlapping with his thoughts. Once, he had looked in the mirror and his eyes had become a strange yellow color, the roots of his hair vaguely white. Once, his hearing had been so acute that fireworks gave him heart palpitations. He had even disarmed his father in training at the age of ten with some strange, alien speed and strength. Medicine, meditation, prayers of cleansing–nothing helped. The only thing that made those terrifying symptoms stop was his sheer force of will. There was a monster inside him and Kauru was determined not to let it out. It took the better part of an hour, but he finally managed to calm down. He returned to the bridal chamber and fell asleep, exhausted.

The next few years passed quietly. Minori gave birth to a son from the handful of times they lay together and seemed to be a doting mother. Kauru paid little attention to the child, he trusted she would raise him correctly. He was too busy with his work with the Shinsengumi anyway. Eventually, Minori caught him having one of his attacks, and she sat beside him through it. He was surprised, as he had never shown her kindness. Courtesy and respect, of course, but never kindness. The shadow inside of him scared him enough that he never got close to anyone. He feared what he would do if he ever lost control.

One day, after coming home with a minor injury, he heard his son was sick with a heavy fever. His wife had also collapsed from looking after him. He had her removed from the boy's bedroom and took over his care himself. The maids were all exhausted. He took a cloth, dipped it in cold water and wrung it out, sucking in air quietly as his wound twisted beneath the bandages on his forearm. He wiped the sweat from the boy's small body–he was only four after all. His name was Suki, which made him suppress a small smile. It meant loved one. At least he was loved by his mother. Kauru wasn't sure he knew what it meant to love, or even hold affection for someone. The child stirred and peeled his dark eyes open slightly.

"Father?" He croaked in his small hoarse voice. Kauru placed his large, calloused hand over the boy's eyes.

"I am here. Sleep now, child." The boy's breathing evened, and Kauru sat back, crossing his arms as he watched him sleep. Softly, he began to hum a tune. He didn't know where he'd heard it–perhaps his own mother sang it once when he was small and sick.

His son grew to be a strong boy and took after him in the way of the sword. When he was fifteen, he joined the Shinsengumi too. Kauru was indifferent to the decision, but seeing how his comrades reacted, he supposed it was a good thing. However, when he found his wife in tears, he thought maybe not. That night, he went to speak to Suki. They sat out in the garden, listening to the frogs and crickets sing in the night air.

"Why did you join?" Kauru asked flatly. Suki flinched, and Kauru took that as a sign to adjust his tone.

"Because A good son should follow in his father's footsteps." Suki replied, looking him in the eyes. He had Minori's eyes.

"Would you do anything your grandfather told you to?" Kauru snorted. He knew his father's words even from his own son's mouth.

"I believe he's right!" Suki protested. "Besides, the work the Shinsengumi do is important."

Kauru didn't deny that. "You should be studying to be heir and manage the territory." Kauru said. "You needn't do something so dangerous just to win your grandfather's approval. There are other ways." Suki grew quiet for a moment, before mumbling something. "What?"

"I said, I'm doing it to win your approval, father!" Suki stood, turning to face him. His face was scrunched up in anger. "You've never once acknowledged me as your son! What else am I supposed to do!?" Kauru blinked, thinking his words over.

"Of course you are my son." He replied blankly. "Has someone said otherwise?" Though he could guess what had happened. The main heir to the Ito family was not doted upon by his father, so rumors were bound to spread. "You should not put so much stock in what others say."

Suki stamped his foot and cried out in frustration. "I don't care what they say, father! I care what you think!" Kauru didn't understand why his emotions seemed to be so erratic.

"I think," he said "That you are my son and heir. Just as I think that your mother is my wife and the lady of house Ito. What else is there to think?"

"Is that really all you think of us?" Suki asked, tears beginning to fall from his eyes. Kauru tilted his head, puzzled.

"What else is there to think?" He asked again. Suki let out a frustrated yell and stomped away, crying. Kauru blinked after him, confused. What had any of that to do with why he made that decision?

The next few weeks were relatively quiet, which was ideal for showing Suki how the group operated. They kept him doing menial tasks for a few days while he learned the protocols, then let him shadow Kauru's unit as they patrolled the city. One night, they were given a tip that a group of Ronin were hiding in the Ikedaya Inn. Suki was with them when his unit was called upon to storm the building. Kauru called Suki up to walk with him at the front.

"You will stay next to me." He ordered, looking seriously into his son's young face. He was excited for his first battle.

"Yes, father." He said almost dismissively.

"Suki." The boy's head snapped around; his eyes wide. It was the first time in years his father had addressed him by name. "Listen to me carefully. You will stay next to me. Do not treat taking a man's life so lightly, for that is what we must do. Do you understand?" The boy nodded his head somberly.

"Yes, father." The group crouched down as they approached the inn, motioning civilians away. With a yell, they broke down the door and began to fight the Ronin. The battle was chaotic, several men storming up the stairs and workers scrambling out of the way. They were certainly skilled; Kauru found himself struggling after the third man he cut down. He was distracted by a cry–his head whipped around to spot Suki fighting a man twice his size. His opponent took the opportunity to strike, and he felt the blade slice through his flesh. He fell forward onto his knees, using his katana to hold himself up. With his second blade he whipped around and took the man out at the knees before severing his head when he was upon the floor. Before he could turn back to his son, the Inn burst into flames. That added to the chaos, and as he struggled to stand, he searched.

"Suki! Suki! Answer me!" he called over the noise.

"Here!" The faint reply drew his eyes, and he found him unharmed, the man dead on the floor at his feet. Kauru began to make his way towards the boy, when Suki's strangled cry alerted him too late. He felt another blade slash his back, cutting deeper than before. The smell of blood mixed with the smell of smoke as he went crashing down onto the floor. Kauru knew he would not survive much longer. As the world began to darken from his view, and the sounds of battle rang in his ears, he wished his son had not joined him.

* * *

Rinkami woke with a strangled scream, shooting up in her futon and starling the monk beside her. As she looked around wildly, he rested a hand on her shoulder.

"It's alright, child, you're safe. Your fever just broke." Her heart began to calm as memories flooded back to her. Her parents had taken her to a mountain temple for fresh air and traditional medicine after doctors failed to break her rising fever. She'd had such strange, terrifying dreams while she'd slept. The monk coaxed her back down after she'd drank some water and assured her that he'd be there when she woke again.

After Rinkami had fallen asleep, he went to the door and called for assistance. The monk ordered for food to be brought up in a few hours, as well as a new futon and a change of clothes. The bhikkhuni bowed and turned to do his bidding. He closed the door and observed her from where he stood. While sleeping she looked like any other teenager. But he had seen those ghosts come from her–and return to her body one by one. He wondered just what she was experiencing in that tormented, fitful sleep she had displayed. Was she really reliving four lifetimes? Could such a young body and mind really withstand that kind of pressure? He supposed only time would tell. He came back to sit beside her and saw her sleep was peaceful this time. Good. She would need much more rest to recover. The monk wondered if her parents knew of her condition when they named her "Little God".

## *Welcoming*

The moon was out in full that night. It was the ideal time to bring a new witch into the coven. The forest rustled around them as they walked. The elder walked in front, she wore a dark dress covered by a robe. Behind her was a younger woman in white, looking excited and nervous.

After a little ways down the footpath a member of the Coven, the Challenger, stepped forward. She wore a mask decorated like a shield, and from within her own cloak she pulled a short sword. The hilt was decorated with garnets that glittered in the dappled moonlight.

"Who comes to the gate?"

"It is I, the Herbalist, child of earth and starry heaven." Responded the young woman.

"Who speaks for you?" The Challenger asked, looking at the woman beside her.

"It is I, the Illusionist, who vouches for her."

The Challenger holds the point of the sword up to the candidate's heart.

"You are about to enter a vortex of power, a place beyond imagining, where birth and death, dark and light, joy and pain, meet and make one. You are about to step between the worlds, beyond time, outside the realm of your human life. You who stand on the threshold of the dread Mighty

Ones, have you the courage to make the attempt?
For know it is better to fall on my blade and perish
than to make the attempt with fear in thy heart!"

The apprentice answered. "I tread the path
with perfect love and perfect trust."

"Prepare for death and rebirth." The
Challenger replied. She lifted her blade and with a
clean, practiced slice, cut away her dress. The
apprentice stood before them bare, and the
Illusionist stepped back. The Challenger thrust her
sword into the earth by the path. The trees around
them shook in the wind. She blindfolded the
apprentice, then bound her wrists and wrapped cord
around one ankle.

"And She was bound as all living things
must be, who would enter the Kingdom of Death.
And Her feet were neither bound nor free." The
challenger led the apprentice to a tub and bathed
her, while still blindfolded. The coven took turns
cupping water over her body as she was bathed. She
was helped from the tub and dried off. She was
given a clean linen robe to wear.

The apprentice was carried to the Circle.
Everyone in the Coven, starting with the High
Priestess, kissed her brow and said:

"Thus are all first brought into the world,
and thus are all first brought into the Coven." The
High Priestess then led her to each of the four

corners and introduced her to the Guardians, one by one.

"Hail Guardians of the Watchtowers of the East and all the Mighty Ones of the Craft. Behold the Herbalist who will now be made Priestess and Witch."

"Hail Guardians of the Watchtowers of the West and all the Mighty Ones of the Craft. Behold the Herbalist who will now be made Priestess and Witch."

"Hail Guardians of the Watchtowers of the South and all the Mighty Ones of the Craft. Behold the Herbalist who will now be made Priestess and Witch."

"Hail Guardians of the Watchtowers of the North and all the Mighty Ones of the Craft. Behold the Herbalist who will now be made Priestess and Witch."

The High Priestess brought her back to the altar, where she stood before the coven. She placed another kiss upon the apprentice's brow and placed a light touch upon each area as she spoke." Blessed be thy feet, that have brought thee in these ways. Blessed be thy knees, that shall kneel at the sacred altar. Blessed be thy womb, without which we would not be. Blessed be thy chest, formed in beauty. Blessed be thy lips, that shall utter the Sacred Names." The herbalist opened her eyes as the chant ended. "Are you willing to swear the oath?" The high priestess asked.

"I am." She replied.

"Are you willing to suffer to learn?"

"Yes."

The High Priestess took her hand and with a needle properly purified by fire and water, pricked her finger, squeezing a few drops out onto the measure. The apprentice then knelt and placed one hand on her head and the other beneath her heel and she repeated what she had memorized for this moment. "I will not reveal the whereabouts or identities of our people until specifically asked to do so, and I will keep secret whatever that is requested of me. I vow to study magic and become an expert in the craft, but I will never, under any circumstances, use magic to deceive or harm others. That I shall lend my support to the Wise Craft and protect its reputation with the utmost seriousness. It is my sincere intention to hold these promises in the highest regard, as if they had been made before the Elder Gods. I am willing to face the consequences that come with dishonoring the faith and confidence that others have placed in me. In this life or the next, I know that no one can run away from the blessings or curses that they bring upon themselves."

"Repeat after me," Instructed the High priestess.

'I, the Herbalist, do of my own free will swear to protect, help and defend my sisters and brothers of the Art and to keep the Coven's Charge. I will always keep secrets that must not be revealed. I swear on my mother's womb and my hopes of future lives, mindful that my measure has been taken, and in the presence of the Mighty Ones. All between my two hands belongs to the Goddess."

The High Priestess made an X mark on the initiate's forehead.

"May your mind be free. May your heart be free. May your body be free. I give you the Craft name of the Herbalist." The rest of the Coven members grabbed her suddenly, lifted her and carried her three times around the Circle, laughing and shrieking. They placed her down on the altar and chanted her new name. The blindfold was removed, and she looked into the smiling face of the High Priestess.

"Know that the hands that have touched you are the hands of love. Thus are all first brought into the world, and thus are all first brought into the Coven. In the Burning Times, when each member of the Coven held the lives of the others in their hands, this would have been kept and be used against you should you endanger the others. But in these more fortunate times, love and trust prevail, so take this, keep it or burn it, and be free to go or to stay as your heart leads you."

The coven surrounded her once more, each woman throwing off her mask and embracing her. Cheers and laughter rang throughout the clearing. The Herbalist wound her way through the crowd until she found the Illusionist, who gave her the biggest smile of them all.

"Congratulations! I knew you could do it." They hugged tightly.

"Thank you!" She responded gleefully. "It was terribly nerve wracking at first, especially with that sword, but once we got to the incantations, I didn't feel nervous anymore."

The Illusionist laughed. "Of course you didn't. You only spent two months memorizing it all from my grimoire." the Herbalist blushed heavily, but smiled anyway.

"So, when do I begin my duties? When do I take my fae incantation? Do I need to tend the wellspring tonight? When will I get my familiar?"

"Slow down, dear." A voice came from behind them. The witches turned to see the High Priestess coming towards them. Most everyone had removed their ceremonial robes and masks now. With it, the elderly witch looked just like any old woman you'd see in the village. Her eyes glittered as she approached the newly initiated witch. "All will come to you in due time. Others will tend the wellspring tonight. Everyone else will be going home, you included." She waved her walking stick toward the edge of the clearing, and the foliage parted. "Get some rest. Tomorrow we can begin the rest." She bid the others goodnight and followed the crowd out along the path that had opened. She continued to follow the Illusionist as the group broke apart once they left the trees.

They made it back to the village and into their shared home without incident. Dressing in her nightclothes, she crawled into bed and turned over to look at the other woman.

"Hey, Christine?"

"Yes, River?"

"I'm finally a witch!!" She squealed in excitement. Christine laughed.

"You've been apprenticing with me for two whole years, River. I don't know why you're so excited all of a sudden."

River stuck her tongue out. "It's not the same! The Initiation makes it real, now! You can't tell me you weren't excited for your own."

"You're right," Christine responded "I was. Now, can we please go to sleep?"

"Fine, fine." River replied. "Goodnight, Christine."

"Goodnight, little witch." River smiled again, feeling joy sink from the top of her head to the tip of her toes.

Llydell

## *Old Gods*

A deer wanders a church in silence, surveying the home of the deity usurper. His hooves echo loudly against the polished stone floor, and his ears twitched at the unnatural sound. Dark eyes take in the shimmering coves of candles below white stone statues. The small granite saints look mournful, blank eyes holding no warmth.

Stepping up to the Dias, he tentatively sniffs the thick, gold gilded tome that rested upon the heaps of soft satin. Looking out into the almost endless rows of pews, he sighed, quietly. Flicking his white tail, he raised his head to the statue that dominated the holy place. Dipping it, he then turned to leave, satisfied with having paid his respects.

Once he was back into the fringes of the forest, his body shifted. As it did, flowers sprang up around his now human feet. His pale skin was covered in robes made of gossamer, his long white hair was braided with leaves, flowers, and small glittering things, which caught the moonlight that filtered through the trees. Large antlers protruded from his head just above his temples, framing his pointed ears. Another sigh escaped his lips as he observed the house of worship from afar. It was no less grand from the outside.

"You've returned." A rumble came from behind him. Turning, he knelt before the new figure, a well-muscled, brown-skinned satyr. Small animals scurried around his large hooves. "Rise," He murmured, weathered hand reaching out to pull the deerling to his feet. It was taken gratefully, and when he stood again their green eyes met. All that the deerling had seen seemed to pass into the satyr's mind and he sighed, running a hand through his dark curls. "I see."

"Pan," the deerling said, folding his thin hands into his delicate robes "What will we tell Asintmah?" The satyr's gaze turned thoughtful. "Well, Freyr, we'll tell her that we are now old gods, indeed."

"Soon enough, we'll be new again." Asintmah appeared before them, placing a friendly hand on Pan's shoulder. The hard wood of her palm was comforting to him. "You know how they are, old friends. Humans are fickle. Their lives are so short they cannot help but create something to hold onto."

"I know." Pan sighed, picking up the deerling into his arms. It changed back into an animal and fell asleep there promptly, causing both deities to laugh. "In a few generations interest will spark. But we will still be weak. So many of us have been forgotten completely. So many friends vanished…"

"We can only use the time we are given, not extend it." The dryad responded. "One day we will all be old stories told only in passing. But while we are here, we might as well make those stories great." Pan smiled, dipping his head in thanks. "I just wish the others could be as patient as us." The other two laughed.

"Keep wishing." Freyr responded. "You know they relied much more on the humans' energy than we did. We, at least, can survive in nature."

"The earth never forgets." Asintmah agreed, stifling another laugh. "They will simply have to learn to wait. The humans will come around again, as they always do. We will have new names, but we will still be the same."

"As always." The three figures vanished into the woods to wait.

### *Hope and Longing*

Rumi produced her credentials at the front gate of the Sapphire Citadel. The guard paled a little before waving her through.

"No trouble, you hear?" The dwarf said, the beads woven into his beard clinking together as his mouth moved. She gave him a cheeky smile as she pocketed the papers.

"I'm just here visiting family." He gave her a wary look as the gate opened to the inner city, and she could feel him watching her as she made her way through. It was refreshing to only be a head shorter than everyone around her, instead of looking up at giants. The clatter of boots on the cobblestone streets was comfortingly familiar. Rumi browsed the market for a while until the taverns started to really open. She found the agreed-upon place, the Miner's Song Inn and Tavern. She boarded her steel gray pony, Brooke, in the stables and untacked him before entering to book a room. Once her room was secured and she'd unloaded her pack and hammer, took her money pouch and headed downstairs. She got a table by the hearth and ordered drinks. Her brother was not one to be late, so she expected him to join her shortly.

Not ten minutes later, the door swung open and Brusimere entered. He was tall for a dwarf, his head would reach the bottom rib of a human male of average height. He wore fine clothes embroidered with silver thread, and well-worn boots polished to shine in the torchlight. Stacks of rings adorned every stubby finger and woven into his beard were beads of copper and precious jewels. The wedding clasps attached to his mustache were now halfway down the length of his beard, and she could see flecks of gray peeking through the auburn hair. That sight reminded Rumi how long it had been since she'd seen him last.

Brusimere spotted her easily, as she was the only dark-skinned halfling in the place. Grinning brightly, he crossed the room and lifted her up off the stool in a crushing hug.

"Rumi! It's been too long! I'm glad to see you've gained weight!" He placed her back down before she could protest too much, and the serving wench came by to drop off their drinks.

"And you look just the same, Bruiser." She replied, grinning as he groaned at the name.

"Really, must you keep that awful name alive?" He complained.

"But you were such a fighter! How can I let your legacy be forgotten?" She responded.

"Blue Sage forbids that be my legacy." He said, taking a drink from his tankard. Rumi had almost forgotten how the quality in the Dwarven city was so much higher than the rest of the continent. Every piece, from the stools they sat on the hearth that warmed them was crafted with painstaking patience and love. Even the feel of the tankard's wood against her fingers felt different. She'd missed it.

"How are Della and the kids?" She asked, taking a sip of her own. Brusimere grinned again, always so pleased to speak of his family.

"They are well, thank you! Always asking about you, you know. Della is crafting a magnificent necklace now; I wish you could see it. She thinks it'll be done in just two more years. Dorlan is taking his entrance into the royal guard seriously, and Garnet is studying trade."

Rumi gave him a shocked look. "Are you and Della alright with that? That's below your caste." He gave a nod, one hand stroking his beard as he thought.

"Yes. Since we're in such good standing, I don't mind her doing the work. She can always fall back on our name if need be."

"Still," Rumi said "It's not without risk. Does she understand the ramifications? Truly understand them?"

He nodded again. "Yes. We had a long talk with her before allowing her to apply to the school."

"I hope she does well, then." Rumi conceded. She didn't want to poke where she didn't belong. After all, she hadn't seen Garnet since her awakening.

"She will." He affirmed, looking pleased. "How long are you going to stay this time? You know there's always room for you at our home."

"I know." Rumi replied. "But I'm only staying a few nights to look for work. Besides, I don't want to distract you from your family time. You're home only a little more than I."

"That doesn't matter but suit yourself." He drank again. "How close are you, now?"

"Five gold away." She said, "One more high paying job and I'll have all I need."

"And you're sure about this?" It was his turn to question her.

She took a breath, trying not to get irritated. "How many times have you asked me that, Bruiser? I wouldn't have been working so hard these last ten years if I wasn't sure about her."

"But she's–" He lowered his voice "a succubus. A creature we don't fully understand that was summoned by human greed. I don't want to see you hurt." Rumi gave him a glare.

"If I didn't want to be hurt, I wouldn't be a sell-sword." She snapped. "I'm going to buy her out of that contract if it's the last thing I do. I won't hear any more about it."

"Alright." he held up his hands in surrender. "Fine. But can't I just give you the gold?" Brusimere had always hated her work. But Rumi could not help her nature. She was born from a story of vengeance. The dirty, merciless work she took on was fine by her. Sometimes, she even enjoyed it. "Where will you go after you free her?" He asked. That was a good question. Rumi gave a sigh, slumping slightly in her seat.

"I don't know. I'm not sure where we can go, where we'll be safe." Brusimere reached across the table to hold her hand. The cold metal of his rings juxtaposed the warmth of his touch.

"We'll find you a place. And you know you're welcome here if you need." Rumi smiled.

"Thank you." Brusimere looked out the window, catching a glimpse of the time. "I'll need to be off soon. Della will have dinner ready."

"Oh! Before you go, here." Rumi reached into her pocket and pulled out a velvet pouch. The heavy clicking coming from inside sounded like rocks tumbling together. Brusimere's eyes widened, and he snatched it from her, hurriedly hiding it in his own pocket.

"Is that what I think it is?!" he hissed angrily. "I told you to stop!"

"I don't go looking for them!" Rumi replied defensively. "If I find them on a job, I pick them up. That's all. I can't just leave them there!"

Brusimere sighed. "You're right about that. But be careful!" When the truth of the dragons faded away into history, the Dwarves obscured how they reproduced. They feared humans would come for their magic if they knew, and they were right. When a Dwarf died, their mana stone at their core simply ran out of magic, and their bodies turned back to stone. The family then chose how the remains were to be divided. Sometimes the iron veins were used to make weapons, or the gems taken and made into accessories. Sometimes they just kept the bust. The mana heart was taken out and inscribed with funeral runes, then buried in a mausoleum beside others. If a dwarf was murdered, however, the mana heart could be extracted with magic intact.

Few dwarves ventured away from the mountains, and even fewer settlements lay there, but every so often Rumi came across an empty mana heart. She kept them to be returned, hoping it was simply a raid upon a resting place and not something more sinister. She tried not to look at them for too long to distinguish the runes.

Brusimere was a HeartSeeker. Anointed by the king and possessing a deep stone sense, he traveled the continent looking for mana hearts buried in the ground. If he found a cache, he would report back and a settlement would be set up. Whether or not it was permanent depended on the number of hearts they found.

"I will be careful." She promised. "Now go home to your wife. Tell everyone I said hello and that I wish I could visit."

Brusimere stood, giving her another suffocating hug. "I will. Be safe, my little sister."

Rumi couldn't help but laugh. "You'll hold that over me forever, huh?"

"As long as you hold on to Bruiser." He replied. She waved him off as he left, then ordered dinner. Tomorrow she would search for work. That evening, she ate in silence and simply enjoyed the buzz of the tavern around her.

* * *

Luckily, Rumi still had contacts inside the citadel. Since her type of work was so specific, she often couldn't find jobs on the local boards like a normal sellsword. It took about two days, but one of her contacts reached out and directed her to a small house within the city.

She arrived, knocking on the door. An elven woman with badger markings answered and ushered her inside. Rumi sat as directed and when the woman sat too, she spoke.

"So, tell me who you want dead." Rumi specialized in revenge, but always listened to the reasons before taking the job. She wouldn't take a life for some petty reason. The woman produced a drawing of a handsome human man, perhaps in his mid-life.

"This man killed my child." She said, her voice low and shaking from anger. "We were raising her up from a foal. It took almost three hundred years for us to find a child we connected with. She was still so young–" Her voice broke, and she had to compose herself. "The laws in the city of Ochne don't recognize elven children until they begin to change. He was acquitted in a human court, saying he was hunting for his family." Her teeth gritted. "There was a clear border to the Elven woods. I saw him shoot her. He and his friends laughed. They didn't–" her voice broke again, her hands now shaking with rage. "They didn't even try to take the body for food, like he claimed. They just left her there. That means they either knew who she was or were hunting for fun." The woman had to stand and pace the room a few times, taking a deep breath. "Please. Avenge my daughter." Rumi had been taking notes in her journal as the woman relayed her story.

"What is his name?" Rumi asked.

"Gareth Manubrium." She hissed.

"And what do you want as proof?"

"His dominant hand." Rumi nodded. That would be easier to get away with taking than a head would be.

"Do you have a timeline in mind?"

The woman shook her head. "No." Good. It was easier to work without one, it gave her time to case the target and plan the attack.

"What was your daughter's name?"

The woman was quiet. When she spoke, her voice was almost too soft to hear. "Imra."

"Alright. I'll send you the proof by courier, along with blood that can be tested to show it's the correct man. I'll expect payment sent the same way."

"Fine." Rumi snapped the book shut and stood to shake hands. Once they did so, she left the house and returned to the Miner's Song. She paid her tab for the room and barn, then collected Brook and began her journey to Ochne. The Sapphire Citadel was quite a way away, as it was nestled into the biggest mountain on the west side of the continent, which lay in the midst of its own mountain range.

Over the following month, she checked her map to see where she would post up to begin conducting surveillance. There was the Elven town within the woods just outside of Ochne, but she settled on the ramshackle goblin camp within the city. It was located right by the slums, which would give her ample place to hide. Besides, Rumi found it easier to communicate with goblins than with elves. When she arrived, she showed the gate guard her fake papers, which had her as a halfling cook. It wasn't unusual for her people to be wondering help, as many of them enjoyed the domestic arts. The guard eyed her warhammer suspiciously.

"And that?" Rumi spread her arms out, gesturing to the open air behind her.

"As you see, I travel alone. I need to protect myself on the road." He looked at her for a short while before allowing her through. "Thank you!" She said cheerfully, leading Brook by the reins. Rumi made a beeline for the goblin camp. Once there, she sought out the trading stall with the widest variety of products. That would be the leader of this group. Rumi placed a silver coin down on the counter, tapping it a few times against the wood to get his attention.

"Hello, Dwarf-kin!" The goblin chirped. He had a squirrel tail and ears, with some fuzz here and there in patches on his body. She smiled and tipped her head in greeting. The nose ring she wore signified that she had been raised by Dwarves, though elves and humans often did not bother to learn the language of dwarven jewelry.

"Hello. I'll be needing a place to stay at your camp, please." The goblin tilted his head, observing her with his large green eyes. She knew that look well. He was appraising her.

"Why stay here?" He asked. "You could stay with the big people. Be more comfortable, yes." Rumi leaned over the counter slightly. Rumi was no longer jarred by their disjointed way of speaking. The hive mind the goblins possessed meant that they were hearing every thought from every goblin within an area. Speaking through that noise made their sentences sound primitive.

"My name is Rumi Swallowfoot. I'm here on a job." He blinked a few times, before vanishing into the back of the stall. She heard shuffling and then Swallowfoot being repeated by several different voices. After a few minutes, he returned.

"I am Grum. We are thanking you for helping Tet." Rumi thought back, trying to remember the name.

"Right!" She said, "He needed me to retrieve his saw arm after it was severed in a skirmish." Grum nodded. "Yes." Rumi was surprised, she didn't know the goblin's connected mind reached that far. Tet's job was by the southern sea in the goblin city of Boiling Bay.

"We know you. You can stay for discounted rate. Three coppers a night. We feed horse for free." Rumi's brow lifted in surprise. That was a generous rate. Almost too generous.

"That seems…kind." She replied, looking at him skeptically.

"You come from good tale," he replied simply. "And you must buy something." Ah. There it was.

"Alright." She took back her silver and put down three coppers, before browsing the items he had out. She picked a sturdy bag, embroidered with a simple pattern. "Here. I'll buy one item each day I'm staying." Grum nodded in agreement, then got someone to show her to her tent. Rumi crashed into the bedroll to sleep.

The next day, she began reconnaissance. She visited the back doors of taverns, stables and even homes where halflings were employed. Some refused to help, some didn't know. Finally, she caught a break behind a bakery called Thealeo's. The fat, red haired halfling baker was on break smoking his pipe when she came around into the alley.

"We don't give scraps!" He barked harshly, sounding irritated. Rumi held up her hands as a sign of peace before she approached him further. She pulled down her hood and took out the portrait.

"I'm not here to beg—for food anyway. Have you seen this man? Gareth Manubrium?" Begrudgingly, she took the parchment and looked it over. He gave her a curious look.

"Why d'you want to know, lass?" Rumi looked him over, trying to evaluate what information to tell him.

"I'm Rumi Swallowfoot." She replied simply, hoping her name carried enough weight that he wouldn't turn her in. The man evaluated her with a neutral expression, before handing the portrait back to her.

"Is that so? Well then, He deserves it if you're the one looking. Hold on." He vanished into the door to the bakery and was gone a short time. When he came back out, the scent of fresh bread wafted into the alley with him. He handed over a scrap of paper with an address scribbled on it. "Here's his address. I don't know any more than that, sorry."

"This is more than enough, thank you." She pulled her hood up and turned on her heel. Rumi spent the next few days shadowing Gareth. He left home at about nine, worked at a tannery for a few hours, took a break, and worked some more until around sunset. He then spent a good hunk of the evening at a tavern a stone's throw from the tannery. Once she'd memorized his routine, Rumi laid a trap.

She'd found him to be a curious sort, wandering off his usual path if something caught his eye. He never strayed too far, losing interest quickly. So, she placed a few coins down at the entrance to a long alley a few streets over and hid behind a few dilapidated crates discarded there. She made a bird call as he approached to draw his attention. The glittering of the coins caught his eye, and after he pocketed the money, Gareth advanced into the alley, looking around for the animal.

Rumi lunged out from hiding, swinging her warhammer with all her strength. She hit his knees, one after the other, and Gareth let out a strangled cry as he fell to the ground. Winding up again before he could right himself, she came down on his left leg, breaking the bone with a sickly snap.

"What are you doing?!" he howled. She'd chosen this spot because it rested directly between two taverns. The noise of the patrons would buy her time.

"I'm here to right a wrong." She replied, coming down on his other leg. He screamed, trying to scramble away from her.

"What? What's wrong? Why are you doing this?" How quickly they forget. She mused to herself. "You knew she was an elf, didn't you?" The confused look on his face remained for a while, until it dawned on him.

"No!" he denied. "I had no idea!"

"So you just happened to wander into the Elven part of the forest? The border is marked so clearly idiots can see it." His face reddened.

"It was an accident! I was just trying to feed my family! Not all of us can survive without hunting for half a year."

"Then why did you leave the corpse?" She spat. He flinched. "You didn't even retrieve your arrow." Gareth's face twisted. "Of course a grubby little runt like you would care. It was still a beast! You can't possibly ask me to believe it was a child." *So he did know.* Rumi unsheathed her dagger and planted one foot on his stomach.

She leaned in close to him and whispered. "This is for Imra, you vile thing." Before he could respond, Rumi plunged her dagger into his heart. She stayed there until he stopped moving, then pulled the blade out before going to work on his hand. Luckily, she'd had enchantments put on the dagger to help with cutting through hard substances. Once she was done, she took a handkerchief and mopped up some of the blood before retrieving only the money she'd left out from his pocket and fleeing. It would probably be a while until he was discovered, but she wouldn't take unnecessary chances. Once she had returned to the goblin camp, she shed the blood-stained clothes and burned them. Wrapping the proof in several layers of cloth and tying it into the sturdy burlap pouch, she wrote down the address of her client and went to find Grum.

"Grum," She asked, upon arriving at his stall "Do you have express courier service?"

He perked up. "Yes, we do! Give package, please." She did so, and he appraised it. "Four silver for same day delivery. Special rate for Sparrowfoot only."

Rumi grinned. "If I make it eight, can you deliver it to me wherever I am?" He thought for a moment. "Ten."

"Deal!" She paid him and went to pack. If she left now it would only take two weeks to get to the western fort, which was her next stop. If they could deliver the gold en route that would save her the time of waiting here. Bidding those in the camp goodbye, she left Ochne that night. Halfway to the western fort, the courier arrived. It was an ancient, scraggly, snaggle toothed cat with wings. He looked as if he'd been shoved down a few chimneys, too. Rumi fed him what she could as thanks and added the gold to her pouch after he'd departed.

Finally! She could free Ness from that hell she was in. A week later she entered the Western Fort and found lodging near the slums, where the brothel lay. Rumi rushed there as fast as she could without drawing attention to herself. It had been seven months since she'd seen Ness. Their letters were infrequent at best, and she was desperate to lay eyes on her once more.

Pushing the doors open, Rumi found the lobby the same as it always was. Dimly lit, full of heady perfume and covered in silks. A human woman was walking by and stopped to speak to her.

"Can I help you, darlin'?" She had the drawl of those who lived in the south. Rumi knew the brothel catered to eccentric tastes, that's why there were a few of every race contracted there. But it still turned her stomach to know that humans did that to one another as well.

"I need to speak to Reginia." Rumi replied. "Tell her it's Rumi."

"Alright! Wait right here, honey." The woman moved away and up the stairs to Reginia's office. A short while later, the woman returned to the staircase and motioned for her. Rumi climbed up and followed her to the office, where the woman was then dismissed.

"I didn't really think you'd do it." Reginia said, not looking up from her paperwork.

"Then you underestimated me."

The human scoffed. "No," She corrected. "I just assumed whatever spell Nessrelle put you under would fade and you would forget. It's quite common, you see. These women are flings–flights of fancy. The infatuation wears off after a while." Her quill stopped moving, and she looked up, putting her chin in her hand. "Well? Let's see it."

Rumi stalked forward, trying to calm herself before she said something to ruin the deal. She thrust the coin purse onto the desk. Reginia opened it, making a noise of surprise when the gold spilled out onto her desk.

"This is not fifty gold." She said, looking up in shock.

"It's not." Rumi agreed. "It's one thousand, one hundred gold. Enough to buy out every contract you have and the building."

The woman looked at her, mixed emotions swirling over her sharp features. "Looking to get into the business? I never would have thought. You know, you could have just asked for an apprenticeship."

Rumi snorted in disgust. "Never. Are you taking it or not? It's more than you'd make here in years." The woman pondered the gold as it slipped through her fingers, counting.

"I could just take it from you, you know." She stated mildly.

"Try it." Rumi snarled, reaching for the hammer strapped to her back.

"Joking!" Regenia replied, sifting the coins back into the purse. "Of course I'll take it. The whole kit and caboodle is yours, hun." She began to rise from her seat.

"The contracts, Reginia. All of them."

"You're no fun at all." She tutted, before pulling out a key from her blouse and unlocking a drawer. Rumi guessed it was magically sealed and would have been stuck closed if Reginia herself was not present. The stack of papers was pulled out and placed on the desk, then Regenia was gone. Rumi took the contracts to the office's large hearth and thrust them into the fire, watching as the flames roared and crackled with blue green light. She stayed until every page was ash, and just as they had finished burning, the door burst open. Nessrelle was at the front of a crowd of prostitutes, looking down at Rumi with wide-eyed shock.

"Did you just–"

"Burn every contract?" Rumi replied, grinning. "Yes, I did." Ness rushed forward, scooping Rumi up her arms and squealing in delight. Tears ran from her eyes and both pairs of leathery, bat-like wings wrapped around her to tighten the embrace. Her tail was lashing back and forth wildly as the crowd behind her cheered and sobbed. Once everyone calmed, and Rumi managed to release herself from her lover's embrace to stand on her own feet again, she climbed up onto a chair and clapped for attention. "Listen up! You're all free to go. I bought the building too, so take what you want, sell what you want. When it's empty, I'm going to burn it to the ground, too."

"Really?" Asked the Incubus, Kylaris, in disbelief. "You're just letting us all go?"

"Yes." Rumi affirmed. "No one deserves to live like this. Especially not bound by those magic contracts. Please, live as you wish. If you're unsure or need help, come to me."

The next month was chaotic. Rumi and Ness had to help many of those who had been chained to the brothel find a direction to go in. Most had no family, or had been taken when they were very young. By exhausting her network of contacts and using every favor she'd accrued for the past decade, Rumi found a fresh start for everyone who asked. A few had vanished into the night with what they could carry, but she wasn't surprised.

Once that was over, they sold off everything that was left inside the building. Then, Rumi kept her promise. Using Ness's fire magic, they burnt the building until it was a smoldering pile of ash, leaving the others around it untouched. The pair stood in silence for a while after, just looking at the remains.

"I'm really free?" Ness asked, her voice shaking. Rumi grasped her hand with her own.

"You're free now, Nessrelle. We can be together forever."

Ness smiled, her pointed teeth poking out from behind her lips. "Really? You mean it?"

"Yes!" Rumi cried, laughing a little.

"Can we travel?" Ness asked eagerly, tears still falling as she knelt down to be eye level with Rumi.

"Yes!" She said again, pressing her forehead to Ness's. The black ram's horns on either side of her head poked at her hand as she caressed Ness's face. "I'll take you everywhere!"

"After, I want to settle down and run a farm!" Ness said eagerly. Rumi pulled away, laughing loudly.

"You and me?!" She asked, incredulously. "Farmers?? Why?" Ness looked to her free hand, clenching it.

"I want to learn how to make things with my own hands. I want to be proud of what I create. Does that make sense?"

Rumi pulled her into a tight hug. "It does." She replied softly. "We'll do it, Ness. Whatever you want, I'll make it happen."

# **Pyrrhic Victories**

## *Odette*

As light crept in through the ruins and the trees, the lake turned gold. Ripples cascaded through the water as a young swan circled, head bent towards the glassy surface. Dark eyes roamed the depths searching for its first meal. All was quiet and still, peace and sorrow mingling together in the air.

Deep in the old woods, there is a woman. She will speak of many things, though most often it is the way to escape. A crumbling castle sits at the heart of the old wood, forgotten even when the woman was young. The broken stones, covered in moss and vines growing up the banisters now offer only a peaceful silence. Before the castle lies a lake, left over in the footprint of the moat. It is bursting with life, but only under the surface.

To meet the woman, one must go there after moon high. When the night is a bruised black-blue and the stars only needle pricks on velvet. She is beautiful, with kind eyes, a sad smile and long hair. Her dress seems to be woven out of the water itself, and she stands upon the surface of the lake.

"Who are you waiting for? Or, what keeps you here?"

Her smile will not change as she answers. "I long to see the people who will never return. They gave everything to make me what I am and knew not what prison they created. They locked me here out of sorrow and kindness, so I cannot hate them. I only love them more." She said,

"Why do you stay if you know they are not coming?"

"I cannot bring myself to leave this place, no matter how badly my bones ache to rest."

"Are you lonely? Would you like me to stay with you?" Her smile became somehow sadder.

"No. Do not stay in this place for my sake. Too many people have sacrificed themselves for me. I will not allow another. When dawn comes, you must leave, and promise me to never return." Though her tone is gentle, the words are compelling.

"Fine. But please, at least tell me your name?"

"My name? It has been so long I feel as though it is alien to my tongue." She thinks for a moment, before replying. "I think it was...Odette."

* * *

The traveler sat before her, wondering what else to ask. Of course he had been curious, but it was a dare. Darren never really expected to find anything in the old wood. Odette seemed to glow, soft and constantly, like moonlight.

"Why must we always come at moon high?" He queried finally, leaning back on his hands and watching as the hem of her dress moved, but the water remained still. "The people who ask, I mean." She tilted her head up to the sky, her ageless eyes unfocused.

"In the daylight hours, Odette is dead." She replied.

"What?" His exclamation seemed to shake her from the daze she had entered. Seeing his expression, she laughed a little. Though Darren felt that the sound had once been beautiful, it was hollow now.

"I'm sorry, I guess that doesn't make much sense, does it?" Thinking for a moment, she rephrased. "I am kept here by a curse. Each morning, when light touches the lake's water, I become a swan. Not just in body, In mind and soul. So, Odette dies with the morning light, and is reborn at sunset." Darren stared at her, unable to speak for some moments.

"Reborn?" He felt a little stupid asking, but he couldn't quite wrap his mind around it.

"Yes. My bones change and grow back into a human's, and my memories return, bit by bit as the night goes on."

"Oh. So, at moon high, you've rememblered everything? I'm...I'm so sorry." The sad smile returned, and she tilted her head gracefully in thanks. "Now, what lies beneath your thoughts?" Darren stared up at her, confused.

"There is something that drew you here, and it wasn't asking me those questions. Tell me, and I will help you, if I can." The boy felt the words surface to his tongue, but if he spoke to them, wouldn't he choke? In a trembling voice, he replied."How do I escape my father, and the graves that keep me here?" Odette's face grew thoughtful, and she knelt before him on the edge of the water. Gently, the woman reached out and touched his temple with a soft hand. She closed her eyes and hummed a little tune, her voice flowing like a river. When she opened her eyes, she answered.

"There is nothing between you and the rest of the world but a farewell. Leave just before dawn and you will catch a caravan heading east." they rose in unison. Gripping his hands, Odette sighed. "Be free, and fare well. I hope you find the peace you are looking for."

Darren blinked back tears, excitement and fear overwhelming him in equal parts. "I hope that you find peace, too, Odette." Releasing his hands, she dipped into a curtsey.

"Thank you, traveler." Darren turned away, at last, and began to walk back into the forest. Dawn would be upon them soon, and he still had much to do.

* * *

"No!! Please, God, please!" The prince clutched close to the frail body of the woman he loved. He touched his forehead to hers, tears streaming from his eyes as he cursed fate. "This isn't…. this wasn't how it was supposed to be! Those words I said, those vows, they were for her! For you!" He cried, holding her tighter, as if his begging would restart her heart. Too late, he had slain the sorcerer. Too late had he noticed the decoy's eyes shone differently, that her lips curved up too sharply. What a fool! All those years apart had dulled him. He was so delighted to finally see her once more that he let all the little wrongs slip past.

"Your majesty?" A timid voice broke his mourning, and he looked up. There, in the clearing, hundreds of people had gathered. The whole kingdom. They must have followed him from the ball. Many were weeping. A serving girl knelt beside him, clutching something to her chest. "Your majesty… is that really?" He nodded numbly.

"Yes." Came his hoarse whisper. She gasped sharply, as if unwilling to believe her own eyes.

"Your majesty, what if," she hesitated, "what if we could save her?" The prince froze, his eyes moving to her cautiously. He dared not hope.

"What do you mean?"

"I--This." She unfolded her hands, revealing a small glass bottle, with a glowing, glittering gold liquid inside. "If we all work together, it can save her." The crowd had gathered around them to mourn, but as he looked, he saw determination in their eyes.

"Would you? Really, all of you?" He asked, breathless. Most nodded, a few even laughed, out of nervousness or excitement.

"You two are the beating heart of our kingdoms, sire." A knight spoke. "We would do anything for you." A female cook spoke up, wringing her hands on her apron.

"Please, sire, let's bring her home, ya?" He smiled gratefully, and they began to follow the instructions of the maid. He placed her body in the water, forcing his fingers to let go. Before she could begin to sink, the serving girl poured the golden potion into the lake. Then, they all began to cry out for her, recalling fond memories or pleading for her to return.

The prince said only one word. And when the water began to glow like a new sunrise, he shouted it at the top of his lungs, arms outstretched.

He called her name. "Odette!"

## *Sirens*

Sirens aren't born. Not like other monsters. When the barbarians came, many women tried to flee. Anything was better than being their slave prizes. Husbands, fathers, brothers, and sons all slaughtered. Become a bride to the invaders or join the men, that was the choice. She was barely old enough to stand. She only had a vague memory of her brothers and grandfather. But her mother was a whaler's wife. Louder and more determined than the barbarians were used to, especially after witnessing a mass execution.

One night, when most of the soldiers had drunk themselves to sleep, her mother led the others from our village to escape. She even took the other women, the ones the invaders had already captured. She led them to the ocean.

There's an old tale passed down from mother to daughter for those who live on the coast: that the gods will protect any woman who embraces the sea. It's dangerous and painful; only the sturdiest survive the process. Sturdy comes woven into the souls of sailors' wives. The ones who watch the sea, waiting. The only catch is that you cannot be afraid. The ocean destroys fear. It can sense weakness, and those who are weak do not deserve its protection.

Many women had to carry each other. Some held children, some supported the elderly or wounded. But they entered the cold brine with fire in their eyes as they chanted the prayer. Anything was better than being their slaves. Even death. Even becoming monsters.

Most did not survive the first waves. Salt poured down their throats; it stabbed their eyes with animosity. The water dragged them down, the current ripped them apart. They were drowning. Again, and again and again. When it was over, the water was full of blood and broken bones. Those who emerged were no longer human. They had scales and spikes, fins and fangs. Their eyes were black like the ocean floor. But They were alive! Alive in a way that was so different from before. They breathed in the sea now. They became it. Blood tasted almost sweet.

Her Mother and four others were strong enough after the change to bury the dead. They could not identify them. One elder, several children, but many had been maids. They were buried on that beach in unmarked graves. They didn't know most of their names anyway. As we left the shore, she remembered coming up only once, to get a last look at her old home. She immediately choked on the air, like someone had closed a fist around her throat.

Eventually, they settled at a reef, far away from anywhere. They learned how to hunt, how to sleep and how to heal. For the older women, it was relearning how to live. But it was easier for the children. They no longer had names. Not in the way they used to. Sirens did not speak like humans; it was a clicking, rumbling language used by all in the deep. Occasionally, they managed to rescue girls from shipwrecks. They had the most difficult time adjusting. Comfort was difficult to give. It was better than death.

Becoming sirens came with a condition, as it said in the song. They had to sing of their loss, their mourning above the water. The voices, battered by the briny waves, were eerily beautiful. Her mother tried to communicate with a ship once. They were enraptured by her voice and tried to capture her and the others. Those who had gone out to the ship died trying to escape. She led the next party out herself. She wanted to remind humans that sirens were, in fact, monsters.

She enjoyed the massacre; paid no heed to the screams of the sailors and their pleas for mercy. This was revenge. Men had taken everything from her before, and then they had done it again. When they sunk that ship in retaliation, there must have been some survivors because more came looking.

They didn't know there was a girl on that ship. After all, it was bad luck to have women aboard, especially for long journeys. When she hit the water, her heavy dress immediately began to drag her down. One of the others noticed, and they flocked to her immediately. The sirens tore her dress away, cutting it off with our jagged bone knives until she wore only her underclothes. Three supported her as they swam to the surface, the rest close behind.

She gasped and choked for air, struggling in their grip. Quickly, they began to sing the song. Her struggling became weaker as she listened, looking among us with wide eyes. Fear, curiosity flashed in them—then pain. As the sea began to take hold, she screamed. This seemed to attract other survivors because a small lifeboat came out from the wreckage. There was no way to rush the song. The sirens continued to sing until the men were upon them, jabbing with spears and swords. The ritual was not finished, but they had to leave her. They dove down, and watched as her frame vanished from the water when she was dragged up onto the boat. She would live on as human.

* * *

Rosetta coughed up seawater as the men hauled her up onto the tiny boat. It rocked furiously with the new weight, threatening to topple over. Finally, it stilled and the four people aboard let out a long sigh.

"Are ye alright, miss Rosetta?" Asked the man holding the oars. She recognized him, one of the shipwrights. There was also the second mate and the cook.

"I'm fine." She replied, trying to keep the tremor from her voice.

"Thas' good." The cook breathed, looking relieved.

"What were they doing to ya?" Asked the second mate, bewildered. Rose shook her head.

"I don't know." Her mind was too jumbled to make sense of it now. All she knew was that she would have drowned if the sirens had not saved her. The cold air finally hit her, and she began to shiver.

"Hold on just a while, miss." Said the shipwright soothingly. "It'll be a few days, till we reach the port." They all looked at each other grimly and he began to paddle. He was right. Three days later they managed to pull the boat ashore, each starving, dehydrated and encrusted with salt. The lighthouse had seen them coming and there was aid on the beach soon after. They were taken to the castle and treated for their wounds, then told their tale to the lord. He sent for her father and fiancé right away, as well as the families of the surviving sailors.

Rose was given her own room and thankfully crawled into the bed to rest. She slept fitfully; her mind filled with the screams from the battle. Even more so, however, were the sirens' eyes. They looked human, and that expression they had while holding her up—desperation? Why would they care about her after slaughtering a ship full of men so mercilessly? And why could she not bring herself to hate the sirens for it? Rosetta had watched as they ripped men limb from limb and tore the ship apart enough to sink it. They saved her life, was that enough to make her forget the atrocities she witnessed?

The next few weeks crawled by at a snail's pace, mostly because she was forced to rest and listen as those in the castle whispered about her ordeal. She didn't mind that they talked about it, but the fact that everyone treated her like glass was irritating. Finally, she got permission to go to the lord's library. She browsed the isles for a while, aimlessly picking up tomes and replacing them on the shelf. Rose approached the homely looking librarian, a thin man who seemed only a few years older than herself.

"Excuse me," she said. He looked up at her with a bright smile.

"Yes, miss? How can I help you?"

"Do you have any books with information on Sirens?" His smile faltered briefly, but he stood up and led her to a far section of the library. Pulling three books off the shelves, he then brought her to a table and set them down. She sat when he gestured, and he opened the first book.

"This is an anthology on monsters. It has a chapter on Sirens, though it's mainly about how to avoid attacks and how to fight them off." He opened the next book. "This one is an anthology of monsters. It will tell you about the skeletal makeup of sirens, what they eat and so on. But I suspect this is what you're looking for, miss." He opened the last book. "This is a captain's log of a ship that survived a Siren hunt several years ago. It includes firsthand accounts of his interactions with them." Rose looked up at the librarian and smiled.

"Thank you very much!" He gave a polite nod and returned to his desk, leaving her to read. Rosetta flipped through the first two books just to get a better understanding of Sirens in general, then moved to the log.

*Season of Longfrost, Day 17, Black Moon.*

*Today was our first battle with the Sirens. They managed to fell a sloop, though we rescued a few of her crew. The water was calm when they approached us. Too calm, like before a storm. They rose up out of the water in a group, clad in sealskin armor and armed with spears made of shark's teeth. As we began to ready the cannons, they started to sing. It was a strange sound. Beautiful beyond compare, like a choir of angels. Their voices were rough and gritty, but soft and melodic all the same. Like the sea itself was singing. They sang of terrible tragedies; lands ravaged by war and famine. Women tormented by invaders and their own husbands, too. Try as we might, we could not break away. It was like a trance. We were helpless until they attacked.*

It continued describing each attack and each song to the best of the captain's memory. She read until the sun dipped below the sky and a maid had to come and fetch her for dinner. Her father had arrived, her fiancé would arrive soon after. They sat at the table, Rose listening to her father rant and rave about the attack.

"I'm so glad they didn't get my Rose!" he roared. "They took my Loretta away from me, too, you know!"

Rose's head snapped up. "What? Father, you never told me that's how mother died."

Her father gave a look of embarrassment. "I'm sorry my dear, I didn't mean to tell you this way. I didn't want you to fear the ocean. You know how much your mother loved it." He reached over and squeezed her hand, his face darkening. "But Sirens kill anything they come across; women included. Savage beasts." Behind them, she caught an elderly scullery maid shaking her head. "Your mother was traveling back to her home country to visit for her brother's wedding. You were still too small to travel, and the journey was long. I had things to attend to in our territory, so you stayed with me. Before they reached their destination, the ship was attacked. Your mother was thrown overboard. After the fight, they looked for her, but only found shreds of her dress and blood in the water." Rose squeezed his hand back. Her mother was always a sore subject for him. They finished dinner and he escorted her to her room. "Don't you worry my dear," He assured "Sir Theo, your fiancé will be here soon, and then he'll be able to take you the rest of the way to his home."

"I know, father." She gave him an encouraging smile. She went to bed with more questions than answers but managed to sleep more restfully than she had since she'd arrived. The next day, she went in search of the scullery maid that had attended the dinner last evening. After searching and asking around, she found the woman taking a break with her pipe on a cliff by the castle, overlooking the ocean. "Excuse me, miss?" The homely woman jumped slightly on her rickety stool, looking over her shoulder.

"Ah, yes'm? How can I help?" Rose came closer and stood beside her.

"You seemed to have an opinion of our conversation yesterday." She spoke. The woman quickly shook her head.

"No, my lady! I wouldn't dare!"

"It's alright!" Rosetta soothed. "I'm not here to scold you. It seemed like you knew something. I just want to know more about Sirens." The woman took a long draw from her pipe and exhaled slowly before speaking.

"I reckon you would, with what you've been through. I'll tell you, but please don't say anythin' to the lord." Rose nodded. She continued "Where I come from, there's an old tale passed down from mother to daughter. There's a song we're all taught. When all hope is lost to you, you take to the sea and sing. It's almost like a prayer, beggin' the ocean to protect you. If it's agreeable, and you're strong enough, the ocean will grant your wish."

"How does it protect you?" Rosetta asked. The woman looked up, her eyes steely.

"How'd you think this related to Sirens, my lady?" Rose clapped her hands over her mouth. "An' seeing how they treated you; I believe the rumors."

"W-what rumors?"

"I've heard that if there's a woman on a ship they sink, the Sirens make her one of them. If they were once like us, it makes sense." She shrugged, looking back out over the cliff. Rose fell to her knees beside the woman, her mind reeling. Is that what they were trying to do? Make her one of them? Her mind was reeling. Getting up, she managed to stagger back into the castle and to her room. Sinking down onto the bed, she put her head in her hands.

Sirens were once women. Women who had lost everything and given themselves to the sea by some ancient and forgotten magic. This fact was kept from men, and only passed down as a secret escape in hopeless situations. So why would they attack ships? If they were running away from human life, why instigate battles? It made no sense. Why turn women they found on the sea into Sirens as well? To save them? To increase their numbers? Rosetta only had more questions. Rubbing her face with her hands, she stood. Rose returned to the library to continue reading the captain's log. Part way through her reading, something occurred to her. There was blood and shredded dress in the water the day mother was presumed dead. She began to get excited, pacing around the table as she thought. What if the Sirens changed mother into one of them? It was a possibility, considering how they had attempted to do the same to her. Their actions were too similar to be ignored.

Rosetta ran from the library, bundling her skirts in her arms so she could go faster, her heart beating wildly. She had to tell her father. She dashed through the halls, ignoring the servants who had to jump aside or gasped at the sight of her exposed petticoat. She skidded to a stop before the door to her father's room, stopping to straighten her dress and hair, taking a few deep breaths to calm herself. As she raised her hand to knock, voices became clearer through the door.

"How did you get him to take her with no Dowry, Fredrick?" It was muffled, but Rose knew that to be the voice of the castle's lord, Dougan. She leaned forward, pressing her ear to the door and quieting her breathing to hear better. A laugh came from her father.

"All I had to do was send her portrait and promise him one of my smaller mines. The little weasel has quite a gambling problem, you know. He's already twenty and seven, so his parents are breathing down his neck about marriage." No Dowry? Rose's brow wrinkled. Her mother had left behind a substantial amount to be used specifically for her dowry. What had happened to it?

"That's true." Dougan replied. "But are you sure about sending her off to such a man? She's only just come to be ten and eight."

"He'll treat her well if there's a possibility of getting more from me." Her father said dismissively. "I'm just glad I could get her a husband so fast. You know daughters are just deadweight, Dougan." The other man chuckled.

"That's true, too. I had three myself."

"Once she's gone, I can finally bring my mistress in and marry her. She's pregnant now and it better be a boy. Lord knows I need an heir now. I'm not getting any younger." They both laughed, and Rose backed away from the door, unable to hear any more. She returned to her room in a daze.

Rosetta never would have guessed that her father had agreed to marry her to such a man. He acted as if he had taken great care in selecting the perfect man for her, and she had trusted him. The letters she had exchanged with Theo were always so tender and kind… What had her father said? Deadweight? Is that really what he thought of her? His tone was foreign, full of cruelty and mockery. And he had hidden a mistress from her! She was a good daughter, she would not have objected to him marrying again, should he wish it. If it made him happy. Twice in a day, her world had come crumbling down around her ears. It was too much. Suddenly tired, Rose crawled into bed. When a maid came to fetch her for supper, she refused.

Her father came into the room later. He sat on the foot of her bed and squeezed her ankle gently through the blankets.

"My dear, are you alright?" He asked, his tone worried.

"I'm just tired, father." She replied, squeezing her eyes shut tightly under the covers. Maybe she'd just had a terrible dream.

"Are you nervous about meeting sir Theo, Rose?" Her father asked. "Don't worry, he's a kind man who's excited to meet you! I'm sure he's just as nervous as you." Her stomach dropped and churned at his sickly-sweet tone.

"No, I'm alright." She spoke. "I really am just tired, father. I spent all last night reading." Lying to him now didn't sting like it used to. How quickly things changed.

"Alright, my dear. Get some rest, but don't go skipping meals again." He warned.

"Yes, father. I won't." Rosetta held her breath as she listened to him get up and cross the room, only releasing her breath when the door shut behind him. When she opened her eyes again, it was morning. She must have fallen asleep just after her father had left. Sitting up, she caught a glimpse of herself in the mirror and was startled that her eyes were red and puffy. She must have been crying in her sleep.

Rose got up and dressed, meeting Dougan and her father in the dining hall for breakfast after a maid helped her apply some makeup.

"There she is!" Her father said happily, gesturing to the seat beside him. Rose obeyed, doing her best to keep her face neutral.

"Good morning father, Lord Dougan." She said pleasantly. She began to eat as the men talked.

"We've just gotten word, Rose," her father said, "Sir Theo will be here in three days' time!" Swallowing thickly, Rosetta gave a smile.

"That's wonderful, father." She replied. Rose finished her plate quickly and stood. "May I be excused first? I've been studying in the library." Her father gave her that same smile he always had, though now it just made her heart hurt.

"Of course, dear. But be mindful this time, alright?" She gave a curtsey.

"Yes, father, I will." She did her best not to seem like she was fleeing the room. Making her way down to the kitchens, she searched for the scullery maid she'd spoken to. The woman was lined up at the counter with many others as they scrubbed, dried and prepared vegetables for the next meal. Rose squeezed her way through the bustle of the kitchen until she was close enough to be heard.

"Excuse me! Can I speak to you for a moment, please?" A few women turned, and several of them jumped once they realized who she was.

"My lady!" The woman cried, looking about in confusion. "What on earth are you doin' here?"

"I've come to speak to you again, if you can manage it." Rose said sheepishly, realizing how much work she was interrupting. She dried her hand son her apron and quickly ushered Rose out the back door into the yard where the washing was hung.

"What do you need me for, my lady?" The maid asked, once they were alone. Taking a breath, Rose smiled at her.

"First, your name. I realized how rudse I was yesterday. I didn't even thank you for all you told me." She gave a curtsey to the gob smacked woman before her.

"Quickly, raise your head!" She cried. "No need for that, now, please. My name is Mary, my lady. You shouldn't have come all the way down here just for this." Rose straightened and looked at her guiltily.

"Well, I had one more question for you, Mary." She confessed.

"Alright then, out with it."

"Can you teach me the song?" Mary clutched her chest, looking around them wildly to make sure no one heard.

"My lady!" She hissed "Don' say that so loud!"

"I'm sorry!" Rose replied, lowering her voice to a whisper. Mary looked stricken at the mere mention of it. "Please, Mary." Rosetta begged quietly.

"Why do you want to know that!?" Mary asked in a furious whisper. "You don't need it, my lady. You're getting married to a young lord soon. You'll be comfortable with him, I'm sure." Mary caught the look in Rose's eyes and gave a sigh. "This isn't something to be used lightly jus' because you're getting wedding jitters, my lady." She scolded. Rose shook her head vehemently. She knelt before the shorter woman and took her calloused hands in her own.

"Mary, I'm not asking lightly." Mary gave her a measured look.

"You still have plenty to live for here, my lady. Your father can arrange another match if he's not to your liking."

"Mary, please!" She begged. "I'm no better than cattle to my father! He won't back out of the match."

"Have you just now realized that my lady?" Mary asked in a concerned tone. "That's all women are to the likes of them. You, at least, will live in comfort. Even if your husband isn't a prince of a man." Rose felt furious tears rising to her eyes. She squeezed Mary's hands tighter, becoming desperate.

"My mother is a Siren, Mary!" She replied. "She let herself be changed! Doesn't that tell you something about my father?!" Mary's eyes went wide, then narrowed. Trying to see if she was telling the truth. She pulled her hands away.

"You're lucky you remind me of my granddaughter." She said, defeated. "This won't be easy. It normally takes a lifetime to learn the song. We have a few days."

"I'm a quick study!" Rose promised.

"Meet me on the cliff after everyone has gone to bed." Mary walked her to the entrance of the kitchen and shooed her away.

***

After learning the song that night, Rose spent the next two days writing it over and over. She would burn the pages once they were full in the fireplace in her room. The night her fiancé arrived, she sat at the lavishly laid table, listening to the three men laugh as they drank crimson wine.

"I am so lucky!" Theo exclaimed for the fourth time since dinner was served, his cheeks tinted pink. Her father and Dougan roared with laughter, both also heavily flushed. She smiled demurely as they toasted again to her beauty and good fortune. Dinner ended early because they had to be held up to walk back to their rooms. Rosetta lay awake in her bed, wearing her thinnest nightgown in hopes it would be the least obtrusive in the water. When the castle had been dark for quite some time, there was a subtle knock on the door. She sprang up and found Mary standing there in her nightclothes with a lantern.

"Mary?" She asked, confused.

"This is not something you do alone." The woman replied quietly, reaching out her hand. Gratefully, Rose took it, and they walked side by side down to the beach. Once they stood upon the sand, Mary squeezed her hand tightly. "Run, Rosetta." She instructed. "Don't look back, and don't be afraid."

"Thank you." Rose whispered, leaning over to hug Mary tightly before turning and running full force into the waves. She fought against the current until her feet could no longer touch the bottom, and the salty water crashed over her head. She was never a strong swimmer. Quickly, she began to sing, before fear could truly grip her heart. It started out shaky, interrupted by the water that filled her throat. Squeezing her eyes closed, she filled her lungs with air and almost screamed it. She repeated it again and again, praying the ocean would listen.

Rosetta almost stopped singing when the pain began to shoot through her. She caught herself, and continued to sing as she felt her body rip and change, the sting of salt burning her skin as blood colored the water pink. Tears fell from her eyes and her voice shook, but she continued. She had no idea how long she writhed I the water, agony shooting through every nerve, until suddenly she couldn't breathe. Pulling her head under the water, she saw her body now covered in scales. She felt her neck and found gills there, then fins to replace her ears. Her fingers were webbed and clawed, and her legs had merged into a long tail. Her nightdress looked strange on such a body. Taking a deep breath, she breached ther surface again, seeing the light from Mary's lantern on the shore as she bobbed with the waves. Rose raised one hand and waived with her whole arm. She couldn't see what Mary did in response, the tide had pulled her out quite far.

Turning, she plunged back into the deep. It felt exhilarating to speed through the water with such ease. After a while she paused, treading water as she now wondered how she would find other sirens–let alone her mother. Since Rose retained all her memories from life, she assumed others would as well. When she tried to speak, only a low vibration came from her. She tried again and a clicking noise emerged instead. Rose continued to ponder when a seal sidled up to her. She looked into its large round eyes and found herself surprised when it made a similar vibrating noise and she understood it. Rose asked where other sirens were. The seal led her along for a time before depositing her by a large coral and rock formation.

Rose opened her mouth and made the vibration again. She waited, eyes scanning the dark water for any sign of movement. Silhouettes began to appear from within the rocks. Encouraged, she made the vibration again. One siren swam forward and inspected her. A sharp smile pulled her lips up, revealing her fangs. The other siren responded and Rosetta's chest filled with warmth as she heard the words welcome home.

## *The Martyr*

"Hold still now, I promise this won't hurt a bit." The teen smiled gently at her patient, her ornate headdress tinkling softly. The little boy nodded, tears still leaking from his eyes. Making his best brave face, he froze in place as she laid her hands over his temples. Closing her eyes, she murmured the incantation in the old tongue.

"I seek passage into the dark."

Opening her eyes, she stood in darkness. She could only reach out to arm's length before hitting the edges of her patient's mind. She smiled in a bittersweet way. He was such a young boy; he had yet to experience life enough to feel deep pain and sorrow. With such limited space, his demons could not be very hard to exercise. She felt a mild sucking sensation begin to envelop her left foot and looked down to see a small, watery nightmare attempt to eat her. It almost made her laugh, but she knew better. Though harmless to herself, this little demon was terrorizing the child. "Different people, different pain" went the saying, after all.

Kneeling as much as she could, the girl transferred the nightmare from her foot to her arm, where it sluggishly began to advance towards her elbow. *Leave him.* She commanded, as the inky curtain greedily swallowed up her soft voice. The demon melted away, sinking into her flesh. Making sure the dark really was empty, she took a breath into her mouth and exhaled through her nose.

Blinking, she returned to the world and removed her hands from the patient. He blinked for a moment, then smiled wide.

"It's gone!! Thank you, Empath!" She smiled in return, affectionately tousling the boy's hair. "Of course! Now, grow strong and earn a good name." Nodding energetically, he bowed and bounded out through the beaded curtain. The young empath had not a moment's rest when three boys, just older than she, shuffled in. One of them bowed and began to speak.

"Empath, please, rid me of this ravenous guilt! This demon is devouring me." She rose a brow, smoothing out her formal robes so the delicate stitching caught the light.

"How do you name your demon, friend?" It was rare for a patient to know what ailed them-- rarer still that they admit it.

The boy's handsome face twitched into something that could pass as sorrow, for a bad actor. "I have been the desire of so many girls, I cannot pick one! What else could it be that haunts me?" Oh, yes. She mused, looking him over with a critical eye. His friends were attempting to hide their laughter. Sighing, she beckoned him closer. Holding out her hand, he placed the tips of his fingers on hers and the Empath murmured. "Show me the shadows that hide in plain sight."

Her gaze misted over, and the boy's shadow rose up to stand, morphing into a short demon with gangly limbs and a cruel face. It was worse than she thought. The guilt had been a farce--though she knew that from the beginning. But this avarice was already waist high and hid its long claws embedded deep into his soul. Breaking the trance as she did before, the Empath leaned back in her chair, taking a few deep breaths. "Go to the brothers." She instructed quietly. "You must meditate with one of the peacekeepers for ten days before I can attend to your demon."

The young man gulped, eyes widening. "What?"

"Go." She replied simply, now worried "Unless you wish to be named Greed." Startled, the group fled, in their haste forgetting to bow. Sighing, the Empath slid down in her chair, rubbing her hands on her face. This was no good. It was barely past midday and yet she was already tired.

The beaded curtains began to rustle again, and she looked up, but relaxed when a familiar face entered. "Alright," the other girl said, swinging the wooden door closed. "Take that thing off. Let me see." The Empath rolled her eyes but smiled smally at her friend. "Keen, we have done this so many times, must you still be so crass?" Keen grinned, beginning to untie the complicated knots on the back of the robes as the Empath worked the headdress out of her hair.

Finally, all the layers had been stripped away, her face had been scrubbed clean of the heavy makeup, and she stood before her best friend in her underclothes. The young Empath's skin was covered in overlapping burn marks of all different shapes and sizes. In some places, so many lay atop each other that her skin had turned a deep, angry purple permanently. Keen inspected her friend thoroughly, carefully applying cold water to the new burns the empath had received that day, then covering them in salve.

"How long did you sleep last night? Have you eaten today?" Keen questioned as she finished, looking up.

"I slept some." the Empath replied truthfully "And have not yet had a chance to eat." Even if she had, Empath would not have eaten anything. The demons living in her skin consumed anything she did, then sucked the energy from her bones. Each day she weakened; but she never stopped taking the demons from her people. It would be her death. Keen clicked her tongue in annoyance, looking over her thinning friend with a dark expression.

"I do not understand why the elders still withhold your name." Keen muttered, beginning to help Empath dress again.

"I have not yet done anything to earn it." she replied "I was given these gifts to aid our people. I have done no more or less." Her friend did not reply. Keen's strong arms steadied Empath's shaking steps as the pair made their way to the bedroom. Empath sighed with relief as she sank onto the bedding gratefully. "Please, Keen, do not worry for me so much. I was born to ease the suffering of others. Trust in our elders and our gods. All owed comes with time." She spoke even as her heavy eyes began to close and felt the other girl's forehead rest against hers for a moment.

"Rest, now." was Keen's only reply.

* * *

There were teeth tearing at her skin, yet she did not bleed. Pain seared through her as they pierced and clawed, hungry for any little piece of her they could get. Empath wished to cry out--to scream for help--but boney, clawed fingers grasped her throat, tightening, slowly. Agony towered over her, its pointed teeth and long horns making her wheeze in fear. It sunk it's claws into her flesh, and she could feel its cold poison begin to spread. Paralyzed with pain, the other demons took their chance. A nightmare engulfed her hand and Empath had visions of the village burning. Screaming roared in her ears and tears began to fall from her eyes. Violence began to crawl up her leg, sparking a rage within her heart. She felt as though she would burst with it. They kept coming; hordes of them. All the demons she had taken from her people over the years swarmed her, sucking out her life. She could feel it but couldn't fight it. The fingers around her throat closed.

Empath woke, gasping for air. She could still feel the demons clawing at her, all the pain and rage and sorrow. Her face fell into her hands and she wept until her eyes ached. Keen had left half of a roasted rabbit and a handful of small berries on a wooden plate at the foot of her bed. A waterskin was placed beside the meal. Empath considered simply dressing and beginning her rounds of the village but decided against it. She could already hear Keen's sharp protests ringing in her ears. She ate until she was full, though the plate was far from empty when she finished. Empath moved the plate to the table at the other end of the room and covered it with a spare linen cloth.

She moved back to the main room of her home and redressed–which took her quite a while longer without aid. Once she was suitable, she opened the door and began her daily walk. Empath would walk the entirety of the village once a day, to see anyone who could not make it to her hut like the elderly or injured. She started from her home and did a single loop, going past the pastures, fields, and river and through the cluster of huts at the center. Empath's walk ended at the gathering hall, where she consulted with the elders about the day's events before joining the rest of the village for the evening meal.

Empath waved at Shepard and his grandson in the fields as they tended their flock. They waved back, the young boy following a lamb as it bounded towards her. Smiling softly, she knelt and held out her hand to the animal. The lamb stopped just short of her reach, where it balked and gave a shrill scream before scrambling back towards its mother.

"I'm sorry, Empath!" The child said, rushing up to her and bowing haphazardly.

Empath shook her head as she straightened. "Worry not, little one. Quickly, return to Patience now. He has much to teach you."

"Yes!" He said happily, turning and running away. She sighed and slipped her arms up the large sleeves of her dress to rest on the seams. They were terrified of her. Empath continued, greeting those she met with a warm smile. Once she made it to the cluster of huts, Empath knocked on the door to one. It swung open, and a teenage girl gave her a small nod to enter.

"Greetings Empath. Grandmother is in quite a state today." She warned. Empath nodded in acknowledgement before entering the bedroom. She eased herself onto the stool beside the bed and slipped her hands out of her sleeves.

"The weather is warm, don't you think, Courage?" The frail woman lying on the bed slowly turned her head towards Empath's voice. Her face was deeply sunken, her cheekbones jutting sharply out.

"It is." She replied. "The sun feels like honey on my old bones." She chuckled. "It's back, Empath." Courage continued softly. Her voice was thin and shaking. She blinked slowly, as if her eyelids were almost too heavy to pry apart. Empath looked over her shoulder and motioned for the granddaughter to enter the room. After she had done so, Empath lifted her hand and helped Courage lift hers to meet it.

"I seek passage into the dark."

The darkness greeted her once again when she opened her eyes. She looked around searching for the ailment. When she could find none, Empath took a calming breath and waited. Some time passed before she spotted it–two softly glowing eyes. Ah. She thought. This one again. Fear was perhaps the demon she had encountered the most over her lifetime as the village's Empath. It was barely visible in the darkness, its body a mere wisp of shadow. Only the pale eyes distinguished it from the curtain.

Empath approached the creature and knelt, so they were eye level. Holding out her arm, she spoke in a low, warm tone. *Come now, you're plagued her enough.* It squeaked and squirmed in protest, bristling. She gave a smile. *I know you are just trying to protect her in your own way. But she will be leaving soon. Your job is over. Let her rest peacefully.* The demon wavered at her words, unsure. Finally, it released Courage from its grasp and whispered over the ground to Empath. Winding around her arm like a ribbon, it melted into her skin quickly. With a sigh, the Empath woke.

Courage had joined the ancestors. Her chest was still, and her body was limp. Her granddaughter, Laugh, had collapsed onto the ground sobbing. Empath knelt, ignoring the burning in her arm as she comforted her. She moved Laugh to the main room and seated her at the table before exiting the hut. Empath found a group of hunters returning to the village and took a pair from the party to move Courage to the resting place.

* * *

"You'll be late for the evening meal!" Keen called out before opening the door to Empath's home. "The elders will be furious if you aren't there for the greetings. Come on, I know you don't want to, but you should try to eat–" Keen stopped in her tracks upon entering the second room. Empath was laid out upon her bed as if to rest, her hands folded over her chest. Her chest wasn't moving. The burns had consumed every visible portion of her skin–her body was a horrible ash purple.

Keen knelt by the bed quietly, numbness consuming her. She reached out to touch Empath's swollen face but withdrew before she did. The elders would need to confirm her death. Still kneeling, Keen leaned the heels of her palms against the frame of the bed and bowed her head, breathing heavily. Tears sprang forth from her eyes without warning. "How could you leave me here?" She asked, her voice barely above a whisper. "How could you do this by yourself? You promised. You promised!" Her chest was tight and hot–it was hard to breathe.

Keen had no idea how long she was there, cursing the ancestors and crying until her chest was sore. Finally, she began to rise on shaky legs. Leaning over the bed, she placed a single kiss on Empath's forehead. "I will get you a name." She vowed. Leaving the hut, she ran to the gathering hall and informed the elders, who followed her back to verify that the Empath had joined the ancestors. Once they did so, others were called to move the body and begin cleaning the hut. Keen volunteered to clean and refused to let anyone else in while she worked.

Carefully, she moved all the personal items her friend had collected by the door to be buried with her. There wasn't much. A carved figurine of her mother, a pair of delicately embroidered ceremonial slippers dyed a deep red, and a woven bracelet that Keen had the matching part to.

Empaths were forbidden from collecting too much. They were tools for the village itself and were to live as such. After the collection of iteams, Keen scrubbed the surfaces of the hut with water and scented oil from pressed herbs. She then removed all linens and clothes to be washed later. She brushed away any dirt from the floors and windows and lit a bundle of sacred herbs and bathed the hut in its smoke.

"Rest well, Empath." She murmured "Rejoin your mother and sleep unbothered." Once she was finished, Keen carried out everything. She delivered the linens into the piles to be washed the next day, then gave the personal items to the brothers for the burial.

That evening meal was the longest of her life. After the usual greetings from the elders, the whole village was quiet as they ate. Once the meal was over and cleared away, the brothers came out to summon the village to the burial grounds. Two open graves were dug side by side, filled with things important to them. Some wept, some raged, but all became silent when the elder Wise lifted a hand. The elders stood at the head of the graves, while the village assembled at the feet.

"Today, we bid goodbye to two strong women as they go to join the ancestors. Courage was beloved and made others laugh many times. She helped build our village with children strapped to her back. She was more devoted than any of us, we will miss her absence here dearly." He cleared his throat and looked down at Empath. Keen had been unable to look away from her. No one would have guessed how beautiful she was, now. How gentle her smile had been or how her eyes shone under the moonlight. Keen hoped that she would join the ancestors looking like her true self. "Empath was a generous woman and worked hard for us as long as she lived." He rested his hands on his fat belly and sighed. "We often name Empaths who push themselves to the limit of their abilities or do great deeds for the village." He cast a look at the other elders before continuing. "But we will not be giving her a name." People began to clamor. He lifted a hand and they stilled, though it took all of Keen's willpower not to scream. "Empath did nothing outside the role she was born to. We see no reason to give her a name. If it wishes to be argued, it can be argued tomorrow." He signaled his speech to be over and everyone approached the graves one at a time to see them once more. The sky was stained red and orange by the time the brother began to bury them. Only Keen and Laugh remained long enough to see the women vanish entirely under the soil.

Keen was at the doors of the gathering hall when the dawn broke. She had joined the brothers in their vigil the entire night, unwilling to leave Empath alone for a moment. The elders did not come until midday and they paid her no mind as they entered. Agitated, Keen wanted to burst in as soon as they settled but remembered herself long enough to be patient. Finally, they summoned her and Keen did not bother to sit or bow.

"You will give her a name." She seethed. "It is her right."

The elders exchanged looks. "We will not." Stern replied firmly. "She did only what was required of her. It would be unfair to those who rightfully earn their names."

"Dying for us isn't enough?" Keen snapped, glaring at them. "It was not even her seventeenth summer!"

"It is a shame she died so young." Strength said. "There will be no one for the next Empath to learn from."

"The new Empath is but a babe." Wise said, unbothered. "We have plenty of time to adjust the stories so she can learn." Keen was shocked. They really did not care for her. She meant nothing to them. As long as she was useful. Keen let out a primal screech, throwing one of the smaller carved tables across the hall before storming out. She returned to the grave, sitting down before the freshly turned soil and cradling her head in her hands.

"What should I do?" She asked, rage and helplessness consuming every nerve of her body. It felt as if she was on fire. Letting out another shout, she slammed her fist into the ground. Keen sat at Empath's grave for some time, anguishing over her broken promise and the pain in her heart. "It may not be enough for the ancestors, but I shall name you if they will not."

Keen retrieved a small chunk of wood from the pile at the center of the village, then came back and sat by the grave as she carved. Hours bled into one another as she worked. Keen was never very good at carving–she had always excelled at hunting which was where she had earned her name.

When she finished, her hands were raw and full of splinters, but the name Devoted had been etched into the wood. Keen came to her knees and dug out part of the grave–deep enough where it would not be disturbed. She buried the name there and covered it quickly, thanking the ancestors that no one else had come to visit. Keen then returned to her hut and collapsed into bed to sleep. When she woke, it was past evening meal. The sky was dark and the eyes of the ancestors lit up the sky. An idea had formed in her mind as she slept. There was one way she could honor Empath.

* * *

Foliage rustled around her as she sprinted through the forest. Keen knew the woods like the pathways of her own heart and easily avoided every protruding root and sharp rock. Her mind was empty as she ran. Faster. The word rang in her ears and thrummed through her skull like a drumbeat. She must go faster. It would be dawn soon, and the village would be aware of what she'd done. The hunt would begin soon. She had left before moonhigh, so Keen was confident of her lead. Despite that, she pushed again and picked up speed as she wove through the trees. She would not risk capture.

Keen had doubled back three times and left several false trails as well. Even so, with the unfamiliar weight on her chest she worried about her pace. Hopefully that would buy her enough time to escape the woods entirely. She knew of four other villages along the river, but couldn't guarantee they would take her in. She aimed to go farther–to a place the village didn't know. With a grunt, she held out her arms and swung up onto a tree branch in a practiced motion. Keen caught her breath there for a moment and took a quick swig from her waterskin. She adjusted the bow and quiver on her back so they sat comfortably. Another deep breath and she climbed up the next branch and took stock of the trees around her. Finding a sturdy branch close to her, she leapt from one tree to the next. Steadying herself, she began the process over again.

Keen was the best climber in the village. The best hunter, too. Traveling through the trees for as long as she could to delay the search further. It was slower than running, but no trail would be left if she was careful and she would be able to see them if they got close. Keen swung from tree to tree until her arms began to burn. It was slower than her normal pace and lopsided as the weight shifted with each swing. She found a thick pine with dense needles and climbed it as high as the branches could hold her. The needles pricked and scraped her skin raw, but she ignored it. Taking out the large strip of linen she carried, Keen quickly fashioned a hammock between two branches and climbed into it with a sigh of relief. She was above the tree line now, and the sun was beginning to breach the horizon. Keen laid a hand gently on the bundle wrapped tightly to her chest.

"I will not let you suffer as she suffered, little one." she whispered to the sleeping babe. "You will live freely from that pain and choose your own name."

## *The Wheel of Fortune*

It was not yet dawn. In the eerie stillness, he drew his first breath. It sent eddies out into the veil and the birds nesting in the trees stirred, then settled. Slowly, a single lantern bobbed down the great temple steps. The light morning mist began to thin, dew spilling off the leaves in the forest—the sound of cascading droplets almost like rain.

The monk made it to the bottom of the steps, composed himself and continued through the courtyard. His bare feet treaded carefully over the overturned stones and protruding roots. Finally, he made it to the center of the clearing. Jamming his lantern staff into a crack between two stones, he sank to the ground between the pond and the small, raised dais that sat at the base of an ancient tree. As the branches swayed in the gentle wind, thousands of keys of all shape and size collided gently as the branches brushed against each other; they tinkled like bells. He closed his dark eyes and pressed his shaved head to the ground before the dais, speaking softly. "Good morning, Keeper."

A gentle laugh met his words, and he began to lift his head. Lithe fingers grasped his hand, raising him back up to his feet.  "Good morning, Jinpa." A warm, raspy voice greeted. The young man who had been meditating, on the dais smiled. Taking a second breath, he sighed and peeled open his devouringly deep, inky black eyes. Their hands were still grasped, so Jinpa assisted the Keeper as he rose. Though the young man was much taller, he leaned on the older one easily as they began back towards the temple, his legs numb.

By the time they reached the top of the staircase, the Keeper could walk by himself. He returns the greetings of the monks they pass, greeting the elders with formal bows and blessings. Once they reach his quarters, he gratefully sinks onto the threadbare pillow on the floor. A freshly laundered set of robes sits on the sleeping mat in the corner, the soft pink and red were the only colors in the room. Two more monks entered, greeting the Keeper by lowering themselves to the ground and pressing their foreheads to the stone floor.

"Good morning, Keeper." They said in unison. The young monk bows his head in reply.

"Good morning, Tel, Kiba." He smiles warmly as they lift their heads. "How has the monastery been this week?"

Tel, who was the shortest, but closest in age to the Keeper, spoke. "Keeper, please. No discussing business until you've eaten and washed." The Keeper smiled, the corners of his eyes crinkling as he shook his head, laughing quietly.

"That is what I promised, isn't it?" He sighed, closing his eyes. "Very well, my friend. I will speak no more of work until you've all had your way with me." The others laughed, then began to eat. Tel left the room, returning a moment later with a small tray of food. Clasping his hands in prayer as the tray was placed on his lap, the Keeper murmured "I thank the Buddha and Tel for this food to nourish my body."

After he'd finished eating, Jinpa led him to his private washroom where a hot bath had been prepared. The light scent of lotus and jasmine floated from the steaming water.

"Are you positive you're strong enough to wash yourself, Keeper?" Jinpa could not keep the worry from his voice.

The Keeper smiled gently, laying a hand on the man's shoulder. "Jinpa, how many years have you been caring for me?"

"All your life." the other monk replied.

"And how many times will you continue to ask that question?"

"The rest of your life." Jinpa replied stubbornly. The Keeper laughed.

"My dearest friend, I assure you, I am strong enough for this. My body is fully awake after our walk and Tel's food."

Jinpa sighed, running a calloused hand over his smooth head. "If you're sure, Keeper." Reluctantly, he left. The Keeper undressed and sunk gingerly into the petal filled water, sighing as his stiff muscles began to relax. Another week, gone.

As a Soul Eater, time always passed fluidly through his fingers. As a young monk, however, he often wondered if he was squandering this life. He had to meditate for an entire week at a time just to be awake for a single day. It was the weight of the secrets that forced him into such a state, he knew that. But it was so different from his past lives, he could not help but question it.

He stepped out of the bath and was aided in dressing. Once done, they began to escort him to the main temple. They discussed the goings on of the temple while he had been asleep. The simple wood and stone of the back temple gave way to painted murals and gold accents. He could already hear the noises of the people thronging outside the gates when he was seated in the reception room. Taking one deep, steadying breath, he gripped his wooden mala in one hand, and motioned with the other for the gates to open.

A sea of people burst forth as the doors creaked and groaned to allow them through. The monks shuffled the people into a messy line and took offerings as they were presented. The first in the line was a small child. She wore a ragged dress, but her face shines with hope. Smiling serenely, he beckoned her closer. She walked carefully to him and cupped her mouth to his ear.

"My secret is that I helped Daddy pick out a real cow for Mommy's birthday!" She bounced a little on the balls of her feet as she pulled away. The keeper smiled as a small brass key materialized in his hand.

"Your secret is safe with me, child." He shared a conspiratorial smile with her before she ran back to her parents. The secrets of children were his favorite to keep. They were full of innocence and happiness. The next twelve hours passed similarly– he listened to the secrets of each person in line and placed the key that held it in a small box. They would be attached to the great tree later that evening. He gave a silent blessing to each person, praying for the Buddha to guide them. When the sun began to set, the crowd was sent away.

The Keeper was helped up by Jin and Kiba, who let him lean on them as they moved back to his room. There he ate and bathed again, changing into his meditation clothes. Jinpa, Kiba and Tel walked with him back up the winding stairs to the great tree. Tel carried the keys, Kiba a torch and Jinpa a walking stick to aid them. They moved slowly, taking breaks as the Keeper needed them. He was already feeling heavy.

The closer they moved to the tree, the heavier he became. His breaths were labored and his steps shaking as they reached the dais. The three monks assisted him in settling down. Jinpa wrapped his prayer beads tightly within his hand, pressing it between his own.

"Keeper…" he began.

"Hush, Jinpa." He replied, his eyes already closing. "This is the path the Buddha has guided me to. I will walk it. I may even…find enlightenment at the end." A wan smile touched his lips. He heard Jinpa sigh heavily as his hand was released. He heard the monks begin to tie the new keys to any empty branches they could find upon the great tree. The Keeper could feel himself begin to slip into the deep, unbroken peace of meditation when light footsteps pulled him back up. It would be difficult to speak now, but he managed to pry his eyes open.

Before him stood an assassin. His skin was pale, and his eyes were a stormy blue, some yellow hair sticking out from beneath his hood. How strange. He thought. *A foreign assassin?* A knife was pressed to his throat and the man's face was close enough to feel his breath through the mask.

"Tell me where Che Lorraine's key is, Keeper." He hissed. "If you value your life." He only had one response to give.

"Can't." It was hard to part his lips enough to squeak out the word. His chest heaved with the effort of it. The ninja's eyes narrowed.

"Liar. Tell me which one it is!" The knife pressed further into the soft flesh of his throat and he could feel the sting as his blood hit the cold air. The Keeper shook his head, fighting to keep his eyes open.

"C-Can't."

* * *

Che looked into the monk's eyes. They glittered in the near darkness of the alcove but showed no sign of fear. Did he really believe his gods would protect him, Che wondered, or did he not care about dying? Was peace with death achievable for someone so young? The monk looked no older than he was.

"What do you mean you can't?" He demanded. The Keeper seemed to be having trouble focusing. Who had trouble staying awake with a knife to their throat? The man's chest heaved as he struggled to speak, his eyelids fluttering madly.

"Can't!"

"Is that all you can say?!" Che spat, frustration boiling his blood. He needed to find that key. And he needed to destroy it. His whole life could be ruined if anyone ever found it. The monk's head suddenly fell forward slightly and Che had to drop his knife to the ground to stop it from slicing open his throat. "What the hell!?" Che cursed. The Keeper of the Keys had really fallen asleep while his life was being threatened. This was going to take much longer than he'd planned.

The monk didn't wake for a week. Others came to check on him daily and a great fuss was caused when they found the wound on his throat. For nearly an entire day, his sleeping body was swarmed with monks scrambling around with bandages and salves. Despite this, there was still no guard placed upon him. It was terribly strange, to leave the leader of their order completely unprotected when he was so vulnerable.

When the keeper finally woke, he was helped down the winding stairs from the inner sanctuary to the rooms of the temple. Che followed him all the way, ducking behind trees and sliding through shadows. The Keeper talked idly with the other monks as they fussed over him, helping him bathe and dress after a meal. Maybe he was so weak because he ate so little.

The keeper bid they leave him, and they did. "You can come out now, stranger." He called softly. Che scanned the room once more before alighting on the windowsill.

"Where is the key of Che Lorraine?" The Keeper sat on the thin bed, his legs folded up beneath him, watching Che with those unnerving, endlessly dark eyes. A string of prayer beads moved through one hand as he silently recited the prayer placed upon each one.

"I cannot tell you, because I do not know." The Keeper replied calmly.

"How can you not know!?" Che cried, before steadying himself and lowering his voice. "You are the Keeper of the Keys, correct??" It would be beyond surprising if Che had tracked the wrong man. Everything he'd learned and observed pointed to this monk being the Keeper.

"I am." The keeper affirmed. "But I never ask the names of those who give me secrets to keep. I cannot tell you." Che wanted to slam the walls in frustration.

"Then," He gritted his teeth "How do you tell them apart?" The Keeper blinked at him, like the thought had never occurred.

"I don't need to." He said, bringing his free hand up and placing it on his chest. "The secrets are a part of the sharer's soul. When they give me the secret, that part of their soul merges with mine. I can differentiate the secrets if I must, but it is no different than knowing which finger is which."

"What kind of nonsense is that?!" Che cried. "What use are the secrets if you can't access them?? Why do you do it? What do you gain?" The Keeper smiled serenely at him.

"I take the weight off their souls. It allows the believers to live unencumbered, so they may strive towards enlightenment. I gain the knowledge that I am helping so many." Che smacked his hand across his own face in disbelief. People genuinely believed that?

"So, you do this just because you can?"

The Keeper gave him another bright, genuine smile. "I was born for this task. What else would I do?" Che sat down fully on the windowsill, dumbfounded. His mission was for naught, it seemed. The sincerity in his words and the fact that threats had no effect meant what the keeper said must be the truth. Che put his head in his hands, trying to calm himself. "Why don't you stay a while?" The Keeper suggested pleasantly. Che's head shot up, his mouth agape under his mask.

"Seriously? What is wrong with you?" The keeper laughed.

"The temple is a place of sanctuary for all. It matters not what you have done or who you are to the outside world. Here, you are a child of Lorne, just as I am." Before Che could snap back, he stopped himself. It wasn't like he could go back anyway. Not with his mission in shambles as it was.

"You would really take me in?" He asked cautiously. In response, the Keeper turned his head and called out.

"Jinpa! We have a guest!" The older monk came into the room, looked at Che unfazed and greeted him with a bow.

"Please, follow Tel. He will give you room and new clothes. Keeper, we will be late if we do not hurry." They both bowed to him as they left. Che didn't have time to process what was said, as a younger monk came into the room and shooed him out, before leading him through the winding halls of the temple.

"You will be expected to earn your keep." The young monk warned. "There is much to do to keep the temple afloat. Cleaning, gardening, organizing offerings, caring for the sick, cooking, laundry. You will be assigned tasks on a rotation with other monks. Feel free to ask questions and take breaks as you need them. Morning meal is at dawn, midday meal is served at half past and the evening meal is at dusk. You don't have to attend prayer but are welcome to." They stopped, and he opened the door, revealing a room quite like the keeper's. Clean and neat, but with well-worn linens. Che changed and followed Tel back through the maze of hallways to a large stone kitchen. He looked around at the monks bustling about, then back to Tel.

"Alright. What do you want me to do?"

* * *

Two months had passed since Che had started staying at the temple. Most of the work was boring and horribly tedious, but strangely fulfilling. Maybe it was the way the monks encouraged him or thanked him for even the smallest task. He'd never had so much positive attention for simply doing what he was told.

He found the work in the kitchen the most annoying. They made meals for any pilgrims and random people who wandered in. It was at least easy to memorize the menu, as they only had what they grew in the field by the temple to work with. Sometimes they could use what was brought as an offering, but not often. Che never entered the prayer rooms unless it was to clean them. He'd spent his whole life without help from the gods–he certainly wasn't going to start cozying up now. Despite his bitterness, everyone treated him warmly, which confused him. It was strange, not being forced to do something.

Finally, he was allowed to attend to the keeper during a session. The only thing he'd been restricted access to the Keeper, which didn't surprise him. He was allowed to speak with the young monk during breaks as long as they were supervised but had no contact other than that. Che had snuck out to speak to the Keeper's sleeping body a few nights, though he wasn't sure why. He supposed the Keeper had that effect on people. He put them at ease just by being in the room. It was not really a friendship, but perhaps something similar. Che found comfort, almost, in the way his endlessly deep eyes watched him when they met. Like he was watching someone he cherished.

Everything about this place was strange.

Che walked up and down the line of people waiting to see the Keeper, collecting donations, and seeing if anyone needed water. It was a very long time to wait. He was allowed to offer elderly pilgrims small wooden stools, though there were only three available. The Keeper gave each pilgrim a smile, clasping their hands in his firmly to comfort. With each person, he gave that same loving look. No one complained about the wait. The whole crowd seemed in perpetual good spirits.

About five hours into the session, a commotion came at the back of the line. Before a monk could see what was happening, several armed soldiers had muscled through. The pilgrims began to panic. Che helped move the crowd to the side of the audience room, away from the men marching towards the Keeper. He saw Jinpa try to rush forward but stopped when the Keeper put up a hand. The soldiers parted the crowd further, making a hole. Through it stepped a tall, fit man with long blonde hair. He was dressed as a foreign noble, gold and silver winking on his vest and jacket.

Che's heart dropped. His father had found him. Steel gray eyes scanned the crowd until they settled on him. Che felt his palms begin to sweat.

"There you are, boy." His voice was a sneer. "It seems I was right. You failed." Che's mouth went dry, unable to speak or swallow. His father approached the Keeper, stepping all the way up until the tip of his shoe touched the base of his stone seat. Without a noise, his gun was drawn from its holder and the cold metal was planted between the Keeper's eyes. The crowd gasped and screamed in horror. "Give me the key for Che Lorraine." He commanded, looking down upon the young monk with contempt.

The Keeper looked back, meeting his eyes with a calm expression. The wooden beads began to move through his fingers as he chanted within his mind.

"I cannot." His father clicked the safety off.

"Care to change your answer now?"

"I cannot." The Keeper replied, before giving him a serene smile.

"I'll kill every filthy person in this place until you give me that key." His father threatened, seething.

"My answer will not change." The Keeper replied, his eyes glittering with some emotion Che had never seen there before. Anger. "No amount of blood will allow me to give you the key. I do not know which one it is."

"Are you trying to trick me?" His father spat, his own anger growing. No one defied him. Che felt his legs jerk forward. He was moving against his own will. He tripped up the stone steps to the Dias, panting.

"He speaks the truth, father!" Che cried. He was not spared a look.

"Is that so?"

"Yes! Please, there is no need for this! No one will discover the secret! He cannot tell them!" His heart pounded against his ribs as he desperately tried to appease his father. The Keeper looked down to him, a warm smile on his lips.

"This is no fault of yours, my friend." He saw his father's lip twitch.

"Keeper, run, please!" He begged. The monk's eyes only shifted back up to his father.

"Let's just make sure he can't tell anyone, then." The gunshot rang in Che's ears, louder than a thunderclap. The Keeper's body fell backwards onto the wall, blood spattering across the stone. His father and their men began to return the way they came as the people began to scream and weep. Che found himself screaming along with them.

## *The Moon and Her Night*

Roderick cursed his luck. Out of all the squires, he had to be picked. If he completed his mission, of course, he would be lauded with praise and knighthood. But his mission was nigh impossible for a real knight, let alone a knave like him. Shaking his head free of self-pity, he focused on the map in his hand.

It would take a few more days until he reached the center of the forest. He'd packed plenty of rations, but the stillness of the woods around him was unnerving. There was no rustling of small animals or birdsong. Not even an owl hoot at night. It was well known that there were no predators in these woods, but Roderick couldn't help being on edge. He hardly slept while he traveled through the forest and jumped at the sound of a strong wind through the trees.

On the fifth night, he reached the center of the forest. A half-moon was just peeking over the trees, beginning to shine on the dark, glassy surface of a large lake. On the other end of it was a massive, gnarled tree, whose roots seemed to weave into a cave. At the water's edge sat a woman who seemed to glow. She had long hair that fell about her freely and was dressed in a simple white frock with no shoes. She was looking into the water with a slight smile on her face. Quickly, Roderick tethered his horse at the edge of the clearing and rushed to the edge of the lake closest to him.

"My lady!" He cried "Please, listen to me! I need your help!" He had really found her. Roderick had half thought it was a bluff to prank squires with. The woman by the lake was real, and just as ethereal as she had been described. She looked up at him, startled by his outburst. Withdrawing her hand from the water, she stood. Her face was impossibly beautiful, save for a large scar jaggedly cutting across her pale skin upon her forehead. "I mean you no harm!" he hurried on; afraid she would run from him. He held up his hands to show he was unarmed. She looked at him curiously.

"Alright." She agreed. "What have you?"

"I was told you know where the unicorns are." Roderick replied. "Please, you must tell me! The people of our kingdom are suffering from a sickness that they can cure." She looked unsure, her brow wrinkling slightly. "I know we have wronged the unicorns in the past!" he continued, clasping his hands together. "But more people suffer and die every day! Please, this is our last hope! They can heal anything, right?" The woman watched him as he begged with a pained expression on her face. When he finished, she slowly shook her head, her hair seeming to shimmer around her like mist.

"I'm sorry. I cannot give you what you seek." She placed her hands above her heart. "I have watched, and humans' hearts are still too tainted by hatred and greed. They would return to hunting the unicorns once more."

"Please! I can promise you anything!" Roderick cried. She shook her head again, before pointing to a clump of weeds at his feet. A sprout of coarse grass with small purple blooms.

"That plant grows plentiful in your lands. Tell your healers to mix it with yarrow and holly berries. It will help the sickness plaguing you. That is all I can do."

"My lady!" He protested. Before he could speak again, the water at his feet rippled strangely, as if something was coming up from the depths. He scrambled back from the edge as a slimy black figure emerged. He let out a scream as a Kelpie threaded across the water and onto the mossy ground by his feet. He had fallen over in his mad scramble from the shore. It lowered its massive head to look him in the eye, its own glowing a monstrous red. He shook with fear as it opened its mouth, sharp teeth emerging.

"Go." Its voice was low and rough, and Roderick's body moved on its own. He untethered his horse with shaking hands and fled back into the trees.

* * *

Belladonna snorted in amusement as the little human fled, the stink of fear lingering where he had been a moment before. She turned and waded back into the water, diving below the surface to swim across. She emerged in front of Lorelei, who gave that dazzling smile and wrapped her arms around her nose. Bella closed her eyes at the warm sensation.

"It would be so much easier if you just let me kill them." She grumbled. "Less annoyances visiting so often." Lorelei pressed her forehead to the flat of Bella's long nose.

"There has been enough bloodshed over this matter, my love." She replied "Besides, we cannot blame them for trying. It is in their nature." Belladonna snorted, pulling away and tossing her wet mane from her face.

"Their nature is as savage as mine is. I do not know why you waste your time waiting." Lorelei gave her that smile again, beauty tinged with deep grief.

"Because I must." Bella walked to the hollow of the tree roots and laid down on the soft bed of moss there. Lorelei followed, leaning her body against Bella's side. She combed her long hair over one shoulder and turned her head to meet Bella's eye. "It is what I agreed to, after all."

"Do you think they'll ever be ready, Lorelei?" Belladonna asked, gnashing her sharp teeth together in frustration. Lorelei reached out one thick arm, her hand gently taking Bella's jaw to stop it.

"I don't know, Bella." She replied softly. "I don't know if this body will last long enough to find out."

"What will I do when you're gone?" Bella asked, looking at her lover. Against her own black hide, the woman seemed to shine like the moon, her full face bright. It had been a long time since they were in the same form, but even so human, she was beautiful. Her iridescent eyes that seemed to hold every color at once looked at her with sadness.

"I don't know." Lorelei repeated, brushing her hand down Bella's side. "I became mortal to protect the others. Someone had to close the door behind them. I don't think anyone expected to have to wait this long." She sighed. "I'm sorry you have to see me like this. I miss being able to run with you."

"Better to stay beside you like this than never see you again." Belladonna said. "I will be here as long as you are." Lorelei gave a bitter smile.

"Promise me you'll go far away once I'm gone. Find others to live with. I don't want you to be alone."

"I promise." Bella hoped that it wasn't a promise she'd have to keep soon. She thought they'd have forever when they fell in love. A few centuries were a pittance in comparison. Watching Lorelei grow weaker was torture. But it made her understand why the humans sought her out so desperately. Their lives were so, so short. It was no wonder that they wanted the unicorn's power, they wanted to stay alive as long as possible.

How strange it was, she mused as she laid her head down. To empathize with her prey. Strange, too, to see Lorelei need the things they needed. To eat, to sleep, to need warmth. Such fragile little bodies needed quite a lot of upkeep. "Rest. I'll keep watch."

Lorelei gave her a sleepy smile. "My brave protector."

## *Memory*

The tavern was awash with reeling travelers that day. The cold outside was brewing into a storm, so people were taking shelter when they could. Thorne has busied herself by cleaning a cleared table, her brow furrowing in annoyance at a stubborn spot. Behind her, a tray crashed to the ground. Porcelain and glass shattering caused her to freeze up. Thorne was thrown back into her memory, dragon fire and screaming surrounding her again.

She was hunched under an overturned cart, ruined fruit under her feet. A large hand reached over her and pulled the hood of her cloak up. She looked beside her, clasping her hands together to stop them from shaking.

"Princess, you really have to be more careful." Saul warned, his smile soft even now. "They're looking for you, after all. Keep that hood up and stay close to me, alright?" She nodded numbly at the knight, jumping at the sudden sound of cannon fire. Saul cursed under his breath and placed a hand on the pommel of his sword. "So, they've started the siege, then?" Aurore audibly choked on a gasp, then smothered her coughing fit afterwards with her hands.

"I-I'm sorry." She said, once she had caught her breath.

"It's alright, Princess Aurore." The knight replied. He grabbed her arm with his free hand and unsheathed his sword as they broke out from their cover in a sprint. As soon as they emerged, glass began to shatter above them, raining down and glittering like snow. Cannons seemed trained on them, the whip and crack of the weapons roaring in her ears. Smoke and gunpowder filled the air, so much that the princess felt she was drowning in it. Aurore covered her mouth with her free hand to try and block out the noxious air. By the time they had made it to the edge of the courtyard, enemy soldiers were through the gates. "Quickly, highness!"

Saul laced his fingers together and boosted Aurore up onto a large crate. Others were stacked on top of it, all the way to the top of the wall. "All you have to do is get up and over, Princess! They'll never be able to track you in the forest."

"Saul, I need you with me. Please, hurry!" She reached out her hand for him, feeling as if she was going to finally break down and cry at any moment. The knight smiled at her, that lopsided, subtly sad smile he did when he lied.

"I'll be right behind you. Go, now!" Aurore had no choice but to obey. She began her frantic climb up the stack, splinters pricking her hands and tearing at her gown. She looked back twice, once when she heard the fighting begin--and saw her poor knight surrounded. The second time was when she had reached the top, and just couldn't help herself. Straddling the stone wall, she looked back, and saw Saul take a dagger deep in his arm. Aurora screamed in horror and lost her balance, screaming again all the way down. Then nothing.

"Thorne? Hey, you alright?" The scullery boy's voice shook her out of the memory, and she started as he touched her shoulder. She looked around, a little dazed. The plates had been cleaned up, and the tavern had returned to normal.

"Yes. I'm fine, thank you Boey." The young boy gave her a gap-toothed smile of relief.

"Some customers need this table; would ya mind taking their order?" She nodded and smiled in return.

"Of course. Just leave it to me."

"You're a lifesaver, thanks!" She winced slightly at that comment.

## *Child of Salt*

Boone knew his father was a cruel man, just as he knew his mother was kind. They were opposites in every way, his parents. His father was hard and bitter, his mother was soft and loving. His father scolded him for being childish, but his mother sang him to sleep. He never understood why they were together.

Perhaps his mother was afraid. Or perhaps she dealt with his father's anger for the comfortable life he provided. He was the most successful fisherman in the town, after all. He had three whole ships in his name and the crews to run them, but his own always brought in the most. Boone often found his mother staging out the window at the surf. When he managed to coax her down to the beach, she stood in the sand and looked pained. She would not play in the water with him, saying that she didn't know how to swim.

When Boone was sixteen, his little sister was born. The birth took a heavy toll on his mother, and he stayed home to care for her and the baby. His father didn't seem to care. The baby's name was Pearl. One night, during a bad storm, he sat by the bedside, Pearl in one arm and his mother's frail hand in the other.

"My dear child," She croaked, looking at him with those same, loving eyes as she always had.

"It will not be long now. I'm so sorry I must leave you so soon." His grip on her hand tightened.

"You'll be well soon, mother, you'll see." She gave him a sad smile.

"No, Boone. I'm not strong enough. I've been away for too long." Away? He thought. What did that mean? "Listen to me carefully," She said, as thunder made the house shake. "Your father took something from me a long time ago. A sealskin coat. When your sister is older, you must find it. You must wrap her in it and send her into the sea. Do you understand me? You must. Or she will suffer as I have." The look in her eyes made his heart clench painfully inside his chest. He didn't really understand, but he would do anything for Pearl. He knew it the first time he held her tiny body.

"I will, mother, I promise." She smiled again, looking relieved.

"Thank you, my dear. You were the best thing to happen to me in this life." She reached up, her arm shaking as she pushed his bangs from his eyes. "That is why I named you Boone, you know. You gave me the strength to carry on as long as I did. I am..so proud of you." He watched as her arm fell limp and her eyes became cloudy. Pearl began to wail as another clap of thunder boomed above them. He closed her eyes, then stood and carried the baby to his room. He paced the small space and wept, trying to calm the child.

* * *

It happened when Pearl was eight. He saw the look in his father's eye change.

"I think it's high time to take her out onto the boat." He said casually.

"Father, why would you?" Boone questioned, watching Pearl color on the floor of the sitting room.

"She should know what her father does, now that's old enough." He replied. "And it's high time we hired a nanny and you came out, too. You shouldn't be raising a baby." The business had been failing since his mother died. He'd had to sell off both his other ships to keep it afloat. They still lived quite comfortably, even so.

"Are you sure? She'll get hurt." His father waved his concerns away.

"She'll take to it like a fish out of water, you'll see." That day, when his father left to attend a poker game with a friend, Boone began to tear the house apart. The way he spoke, the way he looked at Pearl had made Boone's stomach sick. He overturned every piece of furniture and dug to the back of every closet. It was in his father's office that he found a trapdoor on the floor under a rug. He opened it, and inside found a locked chest. After failing to find the key, he went and got his hammer, and pried it open from the hinges. Inside, he found a sealskin coat, just as his mother said. It was softer than velvet. He gathered the coat in his arms, then shoved it into a bag and hurried out to the beach with Pearl.

It was a gray, cloudy day. No one was on the beach besides them.

"Boonie, what are we doing?" She asked as they walked to the surf. He stopped, and knelt down to look her in the eyes.

"Pearl, you know how much I love you, right?" She smiled brightly.

"Yes, of course! I love you, too, Boonie!" He smiled bitterly.

"Then you have to listen to me, okay?"

"Okay!" She was a kind, obedient child. The house would feel suffocating without her. Boone removed the sealskin coat from the bag. He wrapped it around her, and before his eyes, she changed. A small baby seal soon sat before him in the sand. She squeaked with surprise, fidgeting. The sick feeling in his stomach grew. He had truly hoped it was a delusion from his dying mother.

"Pearl, don't take it off." She stopped fidgeting, looking up at him with impossibly round eyes. "You must never take it off, do you understand? You must swim far away from here and find others like you." She made noises of distress. Boone leaned down and scooped her up, carrying her to the waves. "I know you're scared, Pearl. But I know you're brave, too. You have to go, so you can stay safe and free." He squeezed her in a tight hug, then placed her down into the shallow water. She turned to look back at him again. "Go, it's alright." he encouraged. "I'll be okay, Pearl. And I'll still love you too, okay? Please, you must go!" She made some noises at him before hopping farther into the water and vanishing from sight.

* * *

Boone had stayed at the beach until late that night, simply staring out at the water. He prayed to his mother, to God and whatever ruled the sea that his sister would be safe and happy. He eased the door open slowly, wincing at the whining of the hinges. The house had been dark as he approached and he hoped that his father was asleep or out. He had no such luck, of course.

The oil lamp on the small table beside the couch flared to life as he attempted to creep to the stairs. Boone braced himself as he heard his father growl. "Boy. Where were you?"

"Taking a walk." Boone replied, hoping he sounded more convincing out loud than he did in his head.

His father scoffed. "Where is your sister?" Boone could see his anger begin to boil over. Should he lie? No. He was sick of lies.

"She's gone, father." Before he could say more, his father was across the room. Boone felt the wind leave his lungs as the older man shoved him up against the wall, his fists balled up on his collar. "You brat!" He snarled. "Where is she? Do you know what you've done?" Boone couldn't help the grin that curled on his lips.

"You'll never find her. She'll be free, just like mother wanted."

His father swore, dropping him and stomping off towards his office. Boone was sure he would look for her. He was sure there'd be hell to pay in the coming days but he didn't care. If the business tanked and they ended up on the street he still wouldn't regret his decision. Pearl was free, and his mother could finally rest in peace.

## *Death*

The seer had just finished locking her shop for the night. Letting out a long sigh, she pushed copper strands back from her face, she'd have to redo her braid soon. Pouring herself a glass of scotch from the glass decanter on the uppermost shelf, the Soul Eater collapsed into her reading chair. Tector slithered up and wound himself around her shoulders. When his forked tongue tried to sneak into the glass, she jerked it away from him.

"Wha'cha think your doin'?? This is too nice to give to a snake." She swirled the alcohol and took a sip, while he hissed at her indignantly "'Sides, you're a rowdy drunk." The two settled down, watching the bright flames devour crackling logs. "Are ya planning on comin' out? There's another chair here for a reason." She called, throwing a look over her shoulder.

Slowly, a cloaked figure emerged from the shadows by the door. They creaked as they moved, very softly, and the weathered hem of their black cloak whispered over the ground. They didn't walk but glided. The semi transparent form eased itself into the chair on the opposite end of the table.

Soul Eater's sharp olive eyes appraised the being, and after taking notice of their lack of weapon, she relaxed. "Didn't think we'd meet like this." She said, "Can I get you anything?" Slowly, the creaking joints of the bone arms reached up and took down the deep hood that shrouded their head. A clean white skull appeared from within, and the bones grinned uncomfortably as they spoke.

"Whisky, if you have it, please." If Death had once had flesh, their voice would have been deep and rich--now it only rattled around the skeleton, dry and echoing strangely.

The seer moved to obey, and as she vacated her chair, Tector sunk down into the cushions, wary of the guest. Any soul who didn't remember Death quailed to be near them. When the woman placed the glass of amber liquor in their bony hands, they dipped their head in thanks, light thrown from the flames tinting the white bone ash.

"I'm thinking you haven't come to take me." She remarked, settling back into her seat. Tec quickly wrapped around her middle, squeezing her out of fear.

"Not yet." Death replied, pausing to sip the whisky "Just came for a chat." The seer felt her stomach clench--and it had nothing to do with the python clinging to her. Having met them so many times, Death was an acquaintance to her. She knew that Death was nothing to fear--for in death there is peace, and hope. Peace, her ever brief rest from life, from her mission. A chance to simply exist, without the heavy weight of purpose. Hope for the new life you continue to have.

She knew their patterns all too well; a chat was never good news. Paling under her freckles, Soul Eater's bloodstained lips became highlighted by the fire. When the woman didn't speak, Death turned his skull towards her, its empty eye sockets observing her almost mournfully. She was gripping her glass with white knuckles, olive eyes latched onto the fire. They sighed, downing the rest of the whiskey in a single gulp. Blankly staring into the bottom of the now empty glass, they said

"Only nine remain."

The Soul Eater closed her eyes, biting down on her tongue so hard she drew blood. Cursing didn't ease the pain, and the blood couldn't stop the numbness beginning to creep into her.

It had finally happened. Her people had dropped into the single digits. There were unholy ways to kill a soul, and the few mortals who believed the myths of The Eaters resorted to them. When they believed, the humans feared having their fate in the hands of another being. Not being able to control their own destinies was both terrifying...and enraging. They feared that The Eaters would all stray from their duties, killing innocent souls because they had the power. The mortals didn't understand. The Eaters were not like them--her people did not lust for power or glory or fame. They did not want for anything--save the necessities, and even those they sometimes didn't need. Their duty was not seen as a gift, but as a prison. To be the grim ghosts of the world--countless bodies with ageless eyes, to know the truth but to remain mute, always tired but never resting--to bring only death and to forsake the ability, the choice to create life.

The Gods, too, snuffed out Eaters souls. They were petty beings, far below Fate, Life and Death, taking revenge for a dead lover or pawn. Sometimes even sending their demigod children on quests, fabricated to make the Eaters the enemy. Unfortunately, they were above her race, and therefore the Soul Eaters were powerless to stop their actions.

A strange sound forced her eyes open, freckled cheeks glistening with tears in the firelight. Looking over at Death, she saw amber teardrops leaking out of their empty eye sockets, one by one. The tears dribbled down the bones, sliding away into the darkness of their cloak. "Life was heartbroken." They whispered, "I could feel them crying." and though the skull was grinning, the seer knew Death was in more pain than she. That was Death's curse. To love the being Life but be doomed to be apart, forever. Death had met her kin--had known them. They not only feel the pain of a lover but the absence of an equal. Fate was a cruel mistress, but everything she did was to maintain the balance of the world.

The immortals look at each other in silence for many moments--The Soul Eater even reached out, and Death took her hand. It was not like when they came to reap, pulling the soul along with an iron grip, but a gentle hold. She could feel every bone in Death's fingers but felt too hollow to shudder at the alien touch. Then the seer blinked, and the spirit was gone, only nine black roses in their place. Rising, she arranged the flowers in a vase by the door, tenderly touching each one before parting with it. She left Tector by the fire and shut herself in the back room to mourn in solitude.

The chair Death sat in smelled of whisky scented tears for the rest of that lifetime.

# **Acknowledgements**

I want to thank everyone who came together to help and support me with this work! I received an incredible amount of help from so many kind, amazing people and I couldn't be more grateful. Felicity Anderson, who thought my first draft had potential. William Bryson and Bobby Jo Anderson, who encouraged me and helped in every aspect of the publishing process. Nathaniel Kreeger, my amazing artist/beta reader and editor. And of course, all my other amazing beta readers and editors; Samantha Boelhouwer, Katrina Custardo, Jeremy Decker and Eeka Dellapolous.

For more stories like this,
visit us at
www.brysonpublishing.com